Cowboy

A Story of Yakima Canutt

By: David W. Huffstetler

BH Becher House Publishing

Chapter One

The thunderous applause silenced, as Charlton Heston stepped to the microphone and said, "Half a century ago, a twenty-two-year-old cowboy with both brains and guts stepped in front of a movie camera for the first time. One of the first things he learned was, uh, that movies should move. And, he's spent his life ever since making sure they do."

Enos Canutt stood backstage, dressed in tuxedo and cummerbund, listening to the Oscar-winning actor describe his contributions to the history of movies, but he couldn't describe the broken bones and ruptured organs that rendered him stooped over and in constant pain. The wild mop of hair that once flared from the bottom of a cowboy hat, while he drove his horse faster and faster, knowing the ride would end in his being thrown headlong to the ground, now lay in thin, gray lines over a balding head. But it remained a head unbowed.

The love of his life and companion for thirty-five years stood beside him, and on the other side of America's greatest cowboy stood John Wayne, America's favorite cowboy. "Well, old friend, it's a big night," Wayne said. "You're the first, and probably the last, to get this kind of Oscar. I'm proud of you, son." Enos took his wife's hand and recalled all the movies Heston recounted - *Ben Hur, Stagecoach, El Cid, Gone with the Wind, Khartoum*, and so many more. And there were the days before the movies, a four-time world rodeo champion, yet his mind reflected on a time long before. He saw a ranch house nestled at the foot of a hill, next to the Penawawa Creek, and an eleven-year-old boy watching his older brother saddle his horse.

* * *

The air was awash with the fragrance of cherries and peaches, wafting from the orchards to the front steps of the house. Horses milled about the corral, and the barn cried for a new coat of paint. Enos sat there fiddling with a broken stirrup, as Alex tightened the cinch on a roan mare named Sally. Their father had enough to do, managing the horses and cattle as well as tending to his duties in the Washington State Legislature. It was the eldest son's responsibility to take their produce to the steamboat and, like today, ride back to pick up the money for their sales up river. Even at eleven, Enos had spent his share of days hoeing, watering, and picking that same produce, but he never got to make the trip to the ship's landing platform. But today would be different. Alex climbed aboard Sally, turned, and called out. "Hey, runt. Come on."

"Me?"

"No, that invisible guy beside you. Of course, I mean you. It's time you got to see how the business works."

Enos was thrilled to go anywhere with his brother, fishing, hunting, anywhere. Most of the time, their parents forced Alex to take him along, but this was his idea, and Enos leapt to his feet. He ran to the horse, grabbed hold of his brother's hand, and swung up behind him. He wanted to tell Alex how much this meant to him, but brothers just don't do that. So, he rode astraddle the big mare, clinging to the back of the saddle. They left in a gallop. After a couple of miles, Alex slowed the horse to a lope and said, "When we get there, you've got a job to do."

"Okay. What kind of job."

"You ain't gonna like it, but you've got to fight a kid for me."

"Fight a kid?"

"Yeah. His name is Elmer Swift. He's the son of the ferryboat captain. He gave me some smart mouth the last time I was there, but he's too young for me to fight. So, I told him I saved my light work for my little brother."

"I ain't never been in a fight before, Alex."

"Well, you're gonna be in one today." He glanced over his shoulder at his little brother. "Don't worry about it. Just light into him. If it looks like he's getting the best of you, then grab hold and jab your thumb in his eye. They all quit when you do that."

"That don't hardly sound fair."

"There ain't no such thing as a fair fight, Enos. You do what you have to. I ain't taking you home a loser."

Enos said nothing for the rest of their ride, hoping Elmer Swift would not come.

But he did come. He slid off his horse a full three inches taller than Enos and ten pounds heavier. "Is that the punk you want me to fight?" he asked.

"That's my little brother, but he ain't no punk, and you're fixing to find that out." Alex leaned close and whispered, "Remember what I told you."

Enos clinched is fists, but he didn't want to fight. His muscles were solid from hard work on the ranch, but he'd never been in a fight, had never hurt anyone, and he hadn't picked this fight. He wondered why he was there, but Elmer didn't hesitate. He grabbed a handful of hair and punched Enos squarely on the nose, sending him to the seat of his pants. And, something happened, an explosion of innate fury even Alex couldn't have predicted. Enos wiped blood from his face as he sprang to his feet. He drove his shoulder into the boy's stomach and pushed him onto the dock. He threw four hard belly punches, and then jerked his head up into Elmer's face. They both fell into the shallow water. Enos stood upright first. Every time the bigger boy tried to rise, he punched him. Three times, four, and before he could throw the fifth punch, Elmer raised a hand. "I've had enough." He crawled out of the water and mounted his horse. As he rode away, he turned and said, "You don't fight fair, boy."

Enos squared his shoulders and yelled back, "Go tell your mama."

Alex waited till the horse and rider were out of sight, then said, "Go tell your mama? What's that supposed to mean?"

Enos grinned. "I don't know. It just felt like the thing to say."

"Well, you did good, and I'm proud of you." They were golden words for a little brother to hear. Alex looked him over and said, "Now, we have to see what Mama says when she sees that shirt.

* * *

The ride back home seemed all too quick. Enos had no excuse to give his mother, and heaven help him if his father were home. He'd felt the wrath of his father's shaving strop many times, but somehow, he never quite learned his lesson. As they reached the crest of a hill, he saw only his mother, and he thanked God for that small mercy. Nettie Canutt stood next to a wooden table in the front yard, her hands working laundry over a washboard. She waited until he dropped off the horse and said, "What am I going to do with you, Enos? It's bad enough that Alex stays in trouble, and now you've taken up fighting too. We didn't raise you to be a hooligan. I hoped you'd do better."

"Me too, Mama. I guess I ought not to let boys make me mad so easy." He couldn't tell her Alex had arranged the fight. That would break the brother code. "I reckon Daddy will let me have it, when he gets home."

"Give me that shirt. I'll see if I can fix it. You go on in the house and put on another one. Your daddy will be home in a while."

Alex made himself scarce for the rest of the afternoon, while Enos passed the time picking pears and grooming horses. But no matter how busy he stayed, his mind was fixed on the beating he had coming. His father's horse strode into the yard, as his mother called them in for dinner. The boys washed their hands in a bucket and took their places at the table. John Canutt was a big man, more than six-feet-four-inches tall. And, his stocky frame filled his chair. "Well, what've you boys been up to today?" he asked.

Alex spoke first. "I rode down to the platform. The money is in your desk drawer."

"That's good. I'll look it over after we eat. Did you pick up the pipe tobacco I told you to get?"

"Uh, no, Daddy. I tried, but the store was sold out." Enos knew he was lying, but he had his own troubles without making any for Alex. "But I'll get it the next time I go. Oh, I took Enos with me this time. I thought you'd want him to see what we do, you know, in case you need to send him sometime."

"Why would I send Enos?"

"Well, in case I got sick or something. He did good today."

John scooped a spoonful of beans onto his plate and reached for a piece of chicken. His steely gaze fell on Enos. "What have you got to say about that, boy?"

"Me? Oh, yeah, I could do it, if you needed me to. I kind of like going."

"Did you do all the picking I told you to do?"

"Yes, sir, and I groomed the horses, too, just like you said."

"Then I guess it's all right for you to go sometimes. Just don't let it get in the way of your chores. Your work comes first." His face softened as he turned to his wife. "What about you, Nettie?"

Here it comes, Enos thought. The busted nose was nothing to what his father would give him.

His mother looked past him to her husband. "Just the usual. I was hoping you'd get me some cloth in Seattle, so I can make some new clothes for you and the boys, and maybe a dress for me."

"I had them ship it, so I wouldn't ruin it on the back of my saddle. I'll send one of the boys to town in the morning. It ought to be in by then."

The room sat silent, but for the sounds of people eating. His mother had spared him, and his heart eased back into his chest. Alex wasn't so generous. "Enos got into a fight today, Daddy, but it wasn't his fault. This big, old boy called him a bad name, and things got out of hand. But he did really good."

John sat for a moment, and then said, "Eat your dinner, Enos. When you're done, get my strop and meet me in the woodshed."

"Yes, sir."

* * *

The bloody nose and strop marks across his rump didn't earn Enos any time off from his chores on the ranch. There was plowing to be done, horses to groom, and harnesses to be mended. He remained angry with his brother, until the day he brought home a horse named Buck. This bronc was nothing like Sally. He had a mean streak that even the man who sold him didn't try to hide. Alex was determined to break him, but it was no easy task. He wrapped a cloth around the horse's eyes, while he saddled him. Once he was aboard, he motioned to Enos. "Come on. Pull the rag off. I'm gonna teach this big boy a lesson."

"Are you sure about this? Maybe you should wait for Daddy to help you."

"Pull it off."

Enos climbed over the corral rails, snatched the cloth off, and quickly retreated. Buck was appropriately name. He kicked and turned and jumped like his tail was on fire. Alex whooped, waving his free hand in the air. "You've got him, Alex. Bring him around." But the look on Alex's face told Enos something was wrong. His free hand flew to the saddle horn. Buck had him loose and ran toward the railing. With one mighty jump, he tossed Alex off, and his head struck a post. Enos ran to him with the horse still kicking and snorting behind him. Blood pooling under his head told Enos that Alex was badly hurt. He dragged him under the bottom rail and ran for the house. His screams brought his father to the door.

"What is it, boy? What's wrong with you?"

"Alex is hurt. That new bronc threw him, and he's bleeding bad."

John called into the house. "Nettie, bring some rags." Then he ran to the corral with Enos close behind. He knelt beside Alex. "My God, this is bad. All right, Enos, saddle a horse and ride to town for the doctor. Your mama and I will do the best we can till you get back."

"Is he going to die, Daddy?"

"Why are you still here? Your mama and I will take care of Alex. You get Doc Barlow and be quick about it."

Enos was young, but he was an excellent horseman. He didn't bother to saddle his horse. He slapped the bit in place, slung his leg over its bare back, and rode full speed into town. The trip was quick, but it felt slow. By the time he got back, Nettie had stopped the bleeding, and there was little else the doctor could do beyond telling them to keep him in bed. Time would tell whether their boy would survive. And, he did survive, but only after two days of lying unconscious and then three more weeks of not being sure who he was. Enos waited until he knew Alex would be okay, and then decided Buck needed to pay for what he did. He took a bull whip from the barn, nailed a board to the side of the woodshed, and went to work practicing a skill he learned when he was six. It wasn't enough to simply beat the horse. He wanted to sting him repeatedly, make him understand what he had done. This would be payback.

After ten minutes of snapping the whip, he heard his mother's voice behind him. "What are you planning to do with that whip, Enos?"

"I'm gonna teach Old Buck how to behave."

"And, you think beating that horse is the answer? Why did you wait so long?"

"I wanted to see whether Alex was going to live. If he'd died, I'd have shot that horse. He didn't die, so I'll give him a good whipping."

She walked to his side and took the whip from his hand. "This is not the way, son. You want to beat Buck because you hate him, and you've got no reason to. He's a horse, and a spirited one. Alex knew that when he got on him, and that horse only did what his instincts told him to do. We're not animals, Enos. Hatred will eat you up." She stepped back. "Look at you. Eleven years old, and you're taller than I am. There's something different about you, different from any of my other children. You've got a fire that drives you, and you've got to find some way to control it."

"I know, Mama. Sometimes I don't even know who I am."

She ran her fingers through his curly hair. "You'll be a man one day, and I want you to be a good one, the kind that doesn't take his anger out on dumb animals."

His eyes welled, and he walked away. Somehow his love for his mother was more important than revenge. But he still needed to deal with that horse.

The next morning, he waited until his father had gone down river to the watermelon patch and called for their hired man to help him. "Come on, Kay. I need you to help me saddle Buck."

Kay's broken English rolled out with a Japanese accent. "He bad horse. What your father say?"

"He knows what I'm doing. We're going to take him out of the corral, so I can walk him around down toward the potato patch. He needs some exercise." His father did not know, and the potato patch was the nearest place with soft, newly tilled ground. Kay held the gate open, as Enos blindfolded Buck, worked a hackamore over his head, and threw a saddle onto his back.

"Why you saddle?" Kay asked.

"I want him to get the feel of a saddle on his back. That's all. Don't worry. This'll only take a few minutes, and we'll bring him right back. Look, if you don't want to help me, I'll do it alone."

"No, I help."

This was the horse that nearly killed his brother, but Enos felt no fear. He'd never ridden a bronc before, but this job needed to be done. When they reached the potato patch, he didn't wait for Kay to ask questions. He swung into the saddle, grabbed the saddle horn, and said, "Pull off the blindfold." Kay

12

hesitated, and Enos yelled, "Do it!" When the blindfold came off, Buck exploded. He jumped and twisted, sunfished, and snorted like a bull. He gave Enos everything he had, but the boy hung on. Dirt from the plowed ground flew all around them, and there was something about that ride, something as natural as the dirt. He was one with the horse and rode him until Buck finally gave in. Enos had won, and he did it without a bull whip. He did it without anger. He felt a swell of emotion, and then he heard his father.

"Get off that horse." Enos pulled Buck to a stop and climbed off. For the first time he saw fear in his father's eyes. He didn't know if the big man was angry or just scared half out of his mind, but his voice was stern. "Are you crazy, Enos? Did you see what that horse did to Alex?"

"I just wanted to teach him a lesson, Daddy."

John walked into the potato patch, looked over the mangled ground, and said, "So, you wanted to teach him a lesson, huh? Well, son, I'm fixing to teach you a lesson." And, they returned to the woodshed, but it was too late. Enos had a taste of bronc busting, and he loved it.

It took a few more days for Alex to be back on his feet, and more time before he rode again, but he never tried to ride another bronc. Not so for Enos. He knew his mother worried that he'd be hurt, like Alex, and even his father couldn't hide the same fear. But their fears were not his, and he knew his time would come.

He attended rodeos in Colfax and other towns, but he didn't watch the cowboys. He studied the horses. Each one seemed to have its own style. Some liked to turn their sides to the sun, others landed on stiff legs, and still others kicked as they jumped.

He took a job with a local rancher, telling his parents he just wanted to earn spending money, but Frank Hanna raised a string of bucking horses and he finally caved in to the young man's constant requests to ride them. At fifteen he helped Hanna take his horses to the Whitman County Fair. And, the featured bronc was Hot Shot. But he wasn't part of the rodeo, rather a side attraction. Hanna announced he'd pay fifty dollars to anyone who could make a qualifying ride on Hot Shot.

Enos sat on the top rail of a fence, watching one contestant after another thrown, and thrown quickly. "Boy, that's some bucker you have, Mr. Hanna."

"He's a good one. We're just using him to entertain the crowd between events today, but I've won hundreds of dollars on side bets from men who think their better riders than they are. It ain't that easy to ride, if you have to follow contest rules. But I reckon you know that."

"Yes, sir. Say, would it be all right if I tried for that fifty bucks?"

Hanna stroked his bearded chin and said, "Why not? I don't see you daddy. Give him a go, son."

"Would you loan me some spurs?"

"Sure. There's a pair on the end of that bench. Just don't get your neck broke out there."

"No, sir, I won't." He climbed down, sat on the bench, and fasten the spurs in place. It had been four years since he broke Buck, but failure was not on his mind. A good ride might open the eyes of the rodeo promoters and, maybe, bring his parents around. The spurs sang their jingling song, as he marched to the snubbing horse and slipped his foot into the stirrup. This was it. What a thrill. As he raised himself up, two big hands grabbed his hips."

"Get down from there." His father dragged him back to the fence. "Are you hard of hearing, boy? Didn't I tell you to stay off broncs?"

"But Daddy, I can do this, and I ain't afraid."

John's gaze ran from his son's head to his feet and back up again. Enos stood an even six feet tall, as tall and wide as a man. And, his father's voice softened. "You might not be afraid, Enos, but I am. I've seen a lot of rodeos and I've seen a lot of cowboys torn to pieces. It's a bloody business, and I don't fancy seeing my son crippled by having some wild horse trample on him." He turned to Hanna. "Frank, has this boy been riding your bucking horses?"

"He has and he's good at it, John. Real good." Neither man seemed to know what to say next, so Hanna rolled a cigarette. As he struck the match, he said, "You can see he wants it bad, John. There's only so long you'll be able to keep him from it. Let me give

15

you something to think about. There'll be a rodeo out at the baseball field over in Dusty in the spring. You let Enos come, and I'll wager whatever amount you want that he can ride any horse they bring."

John pulled off his hat and held it against his hip, as he thought. "I'm against it, Frank, and I ain't never going to bet against my own son. But you could be right about Enos. He'll be a man soon, and I don't reckon I'll be telling him what he can and cannot ride then, but he ain't a man yet." He wrangled the hat back onto his head. "Enos, if you've got time after your chores, you can keep working for Mr. Hanna, but you stay off them bucking horses. Maybe you'll ride in the spring and maybe you won't, but you sure ain't gonna do it in front of a crowd way out in Dusty. You'd need to be closer to a doctor."

"Daddy, have you heard about Mr. Roody's roan. Nobody's been able to ride him yet, but I bet I could."

"I've heard about him, and I heard about Joe Pierce's black, too, and he ain't been rid neither. But you ought to be thinking about some nag that might not chunk you on your head."

"Riding that kind of horse wouldn't prove a thing. I want you to see if I've got what it takes for the rodeo."

"Rodeo? Horses nobody ain't never rode? Boy, you are a caution."

"I can do it. Will you at least let me try?"

"To tell you the truth, son, it sounds like you're a little out of your head to me. He paused and let out a sigh. "We'll see."

It wasn't a yes, but it wasn't really a no. Was his father stalling, buying time till the spring, when he would still say no? Maybe, perhaps even probably, but at least there was hope.

* * *

As the summer ended, Enos learned to drive the twenty-seven-mule harvester, but that still wasn't the same as bronc busting. He yearned to be in the saddle with a capacity crowd cheering his every move. But for the time being, he had to settle for a fishing trip with his grandfather. "Cast it upstream, Enos, and let the current bring it down."

"I know, Grandpa. I'm just taking my time."

"What do you want to do that for? The fish ain't gonna wait all day for you to catch them, you know." The old man sliced off a piece of chewing tobacco and offered it to Enos. "Here, boy, you want to try some?"

"You won't tell Daddy, will you?"

"Of course not. Go on, take some. It'll calm your nerves." Enos popped it into his mouth and leaned against a big rock. "Hey, you chew that like it ain't your first time."

"Well, sometimes me and Alex slip a plug out of my daddy's jacket. He looks all over the house, thinking he dropped it somewhere. He finally gives up and buys some more."

"Boy, you're lucky he ain't tanned you for that."

"If he knew about it, I reckon he would."

Alexander tossed a pebble into the water and said, "Lord, how I love it out here. There ain't nothing better in all of God's creation than sitting by a river under a clear sky. I could lay down and die right here."

"Try not to do that, Grandpa. It's a long way home, and I don't think I could carry you that far." They laughed together, and Enos thought about the things he had said. He loved the outdoors too. Then he felt a sting on his arm and scratched it.

"What's the matter? Did a mosquito bite you?"

"Now, Grandpa, you know we don't have mosquitoes in Washington. It's too cold."

"It gets cold all right, but that don't mean you can't have mosquitoes. Sometimes you get the furry ones. Why, I knew a guy from Mississippi, and he used to talk about the ones they had down there. The called them big blue mosquitoes, and they could drink a pint of blood at a time."

"A pint of blood?"

"Oh, yeah. Every once in a while, a swarm of them would light into a herd of cattle and, when the farmer came out the next day, all he found was hide and horns. They had drunk them all dry."

"You don't say."

"I do say. It reminds me of crossing the plains in a covered wagon. We had the worst case of locusts you ever saw. Ate the canvas right off them wagons."

"That's a little hard to believe."

"Well, it's the truth. They even ate my best hat. I had to finish the trip bareheaded, and I'll tell you, boy, crossing the open country without no hat, well, I don't wish that on nobody."

"You know, I think you might be right about those mosquitoes in Washington. I believe one of those big blues flew up here and bit you right next to your ear and drained every bit of the truth out of you."

Alexander spat into the river and said, "You could be right about that, son. You just could be right."

Chapter Two

That winter was the longest of his young life, and Enos grew another inch. He hunted and trapped with Alex, but this time he was the one leading the way, keeping watch that his older brother didn't fall. They filled the smokehouse with venison, elk, and wild boar. And, through the deep snows and bitterly cold winds, he longed for spring. The thought of breaking broncs and riding the rodeo circuit was no longer a boy's fantasy. It clawed at his insides, robbed him of sleep, and kept him focused on a few buildings they loosely called a town – Dusty. And, at long last, the day finally came, but it came at home.

Enos leaned against the barn to catch his breath, after stacking the wood he'd just chopped, and he heard his father call, "Come on up here, boy."

He wiped the sweat from his brow and answered, "I'm coming." As he rounded the corner of the barn, axe still in hand, he saw his father, standing at the corral with a short, stocky man.

John took the axe and sank its head into the top of a post. "Enos, Mr. Pierce is here to see if you want to ride his big black."

"Really? Well, uh, yeah, sure I do."

"Now, he's a kicker," Pierce answered. "And, he's thrown more than a dozen cowboys, but I saw you ride over at Hanna's place. I think you've got a good chance to be the first to take him the distance, but it won't be easy."

"Hang on a minute, Joe. What makes you think the boy can ride that horse?"

"I'll bet you a hundred bucks he can."

John turned to Enos. His dark, down-turned moustache made him look like he was always frowning. "You can ride him on one condition, son. If he throws you, you never ride a bronc again."

But, Daddy . . ."

"That's the deal. If you're good enough to stay on, then I reckon you'll take your shot at rodeoing. But I won't have one of my children thrown off horses time after time, till he gets his brains scrambled." He held out the reins and said, "It's your call, Enos."

It was the biggest decision of his life, but Enos did not hesitate. He walked into the corral, grabbed the reins, and climbed into the saddle. With a nod of his head, he said, "Let me have him." When the blinds came off, the big horse burst into the air. He was everything Enos had heard he was. He spun and twisted, spending every bit of energy he had, but Enos took him from one end of the corral to the other, one hand wrapped around the reins and the other raised over his head. Once the kicking and snorting was over, Enos brought him around in a trot. He'd made it, conquered the horse no one else had, and his heart brimmed.

John seemed to be trying to hold back a grin, but it filled his face. He stepped to the side of the horse, wagged his head, and said, "Well, are you ready to try Roody's roan?"

* * *

While it did have a post office and a couple of other buildings, Dusty wasn't much of a town. It's only claim-to-fame was hosting baseball games. Most of the crowd had come to see the ballgame that just ended, but they stayed to watch and make bets on how long Enos could stay aboard before being thrown. Yes, he had ridden the big black, but this was a real horse, and the odds rose to five to one. The baselines were visible, but only because the grass had been trampled by boys and men playing the most popular game in America. Sam Roody and Frank Hanna tethered their horses in centerfield. Roody led his famous roan to where second base had been. John Canutt stepped forward and took the reins. "That's a sizable horse, Sam. Has he got much spunk?"

"Oh, he's a bucker. It's not a matter of whether he'll throw your boy. It's just when. The smart money says five seconds."

"I guess we'll see." He turned to Enos and said, "Are you ready?"

"As ready as I'll be."

"Now, son, wipe the sweat off and get on that horse, just as if you didn't know I was here."

"Yes, sir, but I'm glad you are here. At least I've got a ride home if he throws me off."

"Don't get thrown off, Enos. Don't even think about getting thrown off."

This was the widest and strongest horse Enos had ever straddled. He'd been nervous for a week, worried he'd make a fool of himself in front of a crowd. Once he felt the animal beneath him, the anxiety disappeared. He was where he was supposed to be, and he knew it. The roan did his best, and the people who bet on him lost their money. Enos rode to the end, trotted to Sam Roody, and gave him the reins, as he stepped off. "Thank you for letting me ride your horse, Mr. Roody. He's a good one."

"Yes, he is, son, but not as good as the man who rode him."

* * *

Over the next few months, Enos spent more and more time working at Frank Hanna's ranch, and he practiced on broncs as often as he would let him. By September, when the Whitman County Fair opened, he'd raised enough money to enter the three-day, bronc busting event. On the first day, over 5,000 people filled the arena, with more standing outside. Enos had seen that kind of crowd the year before, but he wasn't on the card then, and he wondered if he'd bitten off too much. The show opened with fanfare, roping demonstrations, Indians regaled in Native dress and dancing to tribal drums, and the hollow sound of the emcee announcing each event through a megaphone. It was everything the sixteen-year-old had hoped for.

Little Spokane threw his rider, and several other cowboys failed to inspire, but Bill Oakes rode well. Enos knew he would not only need to make a good ride, but he'd need a horse that put on a show. He drew a dappled gray named Pomp, known to be a feisty mount. There was no eight-second clock. Enos had to ride him until he gave in. Pomp did well, bucking and twisting and flinging spit through the air. Then something changed. He crashed through a fence, smashed into another horse, and fell. Enos landed hard with Pomp rolling over his right leg.

The cowboy who'd been leading the other horse took his arm and said, "How bad are you hurt?"

"Feels like a hot iron in my hip."

"Well, forget about that for now. You best get up, if you want a score." Enos stumbled to his feet. "Now, wave to the crowd. Don't let them see you're hurt."

Pain shot into his back, as he raised his arm, but he wasn't going to let it show. "Okay, I'm waving. Now how do I get out of here?"

"When the other guys start taking Pomp back to the stables, you walk on this side of him. Let his body block you from the crowd. Then you can lean against his side, hang onto the stirrup or something."

"Thanks for the help. What's your name?"

"Dave White, and welcome to the rodeo business. I'll meet you at the stables with a shot of Old Crow and a bottle of Dr. Nepaw's Snake Oil. You'll be ready to ride tomorrow."

"Tomorrow? I was wondering if I'd ride again this year." And, Enos did ride the next day. He was sore and not sure whether to thank Old Crow or Dr. Nepaw for helping him back into the saddle. He rode in pain on the second day and was still sore and stiff on the third day. He pushed the pain into the back of his mind and rode Little Spokane to his first win. At sixteen, Enos Canutt had won best bronc buster, and his rodeo career was in flight.

* * *

That evening Enos helped Frank Hanna move his horses back to their camp in a copse of trees near a pond. He sat on a stump, scraping beans from a tin plate, as happy as he'd ever been. Then he noticed a tall man walking into the glow of the firelight. "Daddy? I thought you and Mama would be headed home by now."

John sat on the ground beside him, held his hat between his hands, and said, "That was some fine riding you did today. You deserved to win."

"Thank you. I wasn't so sure about it after I saw Ben Oakes. He's a real cowboy."

"And, so are you, son. Don't ever let anybody make you think different."

John Canutt was a stern man, not given to a show of emotion, and Enos knew something was not right, but he wasn't sure what he should say. "Uh, would you like some beans or something? We've got plenty."

"No, I ate supper with your mother before she left for home."

"Why would she leave without you?"

"Well, that's why I came out here. I ain't real sure how to tell you this, but you're nearly grown now, so I'll just say it. Your mama and me are getting a divorce. We decided to keep it quiet, because we didn't want to ruin the rodeo for you. She's headed back to the ranch with your brothers and sisters."

Enos set his plate aside. "I don't know what to say. Is something wrong? Did you have a fight or something?"

"The reasons don't matter. She's going her way, and I'm going mine." Enos sat quietly, waiting for his father to say more, but he just stood, pressed his hat onto his head, and said, "I reckon that's it. You and your brothers will need to help her on the ranch. I reckon I'll go to Seattle. Keep in touch, boy." And, with that, he left.

His parents divorcing? No, that couldn't be true. They'd always been together, always been there for him when he needed them. In a matter of minutes, he went from celebrating the best day of his life to grieving for a marriage lost and a family divided.

* * *

There were no peaches or watermelons to pick in late fall, and life on the ranch slowed. But the family still needed money. Enos packed a few rations and his pistol into his saddlebags, mounted his horse, and set out to find something, but he didn't know what. He camped along the roadside for a couple of nights, and a hotel in Spokane lent a much-needed, hot bath before he crossed into Idaho's panhandle. He pulled his horse to a stop in front of the only hotel in Bovill. Two men stood on the sidewalk, and he asked, "Could you tell me where to find work around here?"

"Well, that all depends," the taller one answered. "Do you have your union card?"

"Can't say that I do, but why would that matter?"

"We're organizers for the Industrial Workers of the World, the Wobblies, and we're here to recruit members."

"Well, there ain't much use to recruit me. I don't have a job yet."

"I can help you with that. The Blackwell Logging Camp is hiring, and they'll take just about anybody who shows up. You follow the railroad tracks and turn north at the river. You can't miss it. And, once you get a job, you could be one of our organizers."

"Why would I want to do that?"

"Haven't you heard? We took the men out on strike at the Potlatch camps and got them better food and an extra twenty-five cents a day. They sure wouldn't have gotten that on their own."

"Something to think about, I guess. Anyway, I appreciate the help." Enos followed the direction the Wobblies gave him and came straight to the logging camp. He dismounted, tied his horse to a rail, and entered a cabin marked *Foreman*. "Good afternoon, my name is Enos Canutt, and a couple of guys told me I might find work here."

The man lifted a bottle from the drawer of his battered desk, raised it to his lips, and took a swig. He stared at Enos from beneath bushy eyebrows and asked, "Are you a union man?"

"You're the second person to ask me that today and, no, I'm not with the union."

"Good. The unions don't do nothing but make trouble, and the Wobblies are the worst of the bunch. They burned one of our buildings down a few weeks ago."

"Did you put the law on them?"

"No, I couldn't prove they done it, but I know they did. My name is Pete Buzzard, and I do all the hiring and firing around here. Have you done any logging before?"

"Just the trees we cut and sawed for the barn and a couple of sheds on the ranch, but I'm a quick learner. I don't mind hard work."

"Well, this ain't ranch work, boy." He set the bottle aside. "Look, my teamster quit yesterday, said the Wobblies beat him up when he went into town. Can you handle a team of oxen?"

"I drove a twenty-seven-mule harvester back home. I don't think I'd have any trouble with a few oxen."

"Then I'll give you a try. You get paid on Saturdays. The men go into town on Saturday nights. They've got a saloon and a couple of brothels, so most of them don't get back till Sunday afternoon. It's a tough bunch. Take care of your stuff or they'll rob you blind. We've got three bunkhouses. One has the Germans, the Irish, and that kind. We put the Chinese together, and you'll be in with the Italians."

"Have you got a place I can keep my horse?"

"Stables are down the hill. Just work hard and watch yourself, and you'll do all right."

Night was falling by the time Enos put his horse away and found the Italian bunkhouse, but no one looked Italian. He laid his saddlebags next to his bed, and turned to find a behemoth of a man standing next to him. "Howdy, I'm Enos."

"They call me Big Wallace. We're fixing to go to dinner. We get pie on Friday nights. I like pie."

"That's good to know. I like pie too. Come on, I'll walk over with you." The dining room was little more than tables inside a tent. Enos took a plate, and the cook filled it with a ladle of stew. "This looks pretty good." He sat across the table from Big Wallace and took a bite. The stew tasted more like racoon than beef, but he didn't care. It was hot and filling. In a few minutes, a Chinese man passed by and set a piece of pumpkin pie in front of him. Enos started to sink his fork into it, but Big Wallace grabbed it first and wolfed it down in two enormous bites. "Wait a minute." Enos started to stand, and then he saw the blank look in the man's face, and he took pity on him. This was not the ranch, far from it, but it was his new home, and he'd have to get used to it.

* * *

Enos slept little that night. He'd known worse mattresses, but when the men took off their shoes, the stench was almost unbearable. The odor from the team of oxen the next morning came as a welcome relief. At least he was outside. When the day ended, Buzzard paid him just as he said he would. "I watched you today," he said. "And, you did real good. Why don't you come into Bovill with us, and we'll have a drink or two?"

"I appreciate the offer, Pete, but it wouldn't take long for me to drink this up. And, I need to take care of my money, so I can send some home."

"Suit yourself. I won't be gone too long myself. I'll probably see you at breakfast, but don't wait too late to get there. Cookie don't fix much on Sunday mornings, and it gets cold pretty fast. And, kind of keep an eye out, will you? I still ain't sure them union people are done with us."

The work crew left camp like it was infected. If anyone was there other than Enos, he couldn't find them. He walked down to the stable, groomed his horse, and worked his way back up the hill. He turned up his collar against the wind that slithered between the trees from high on the mountain. The day had run long, and his body ached, so he took to his bed. And, somewhere in the night, he woke. He lay still with the feeling he wasn't alone, and he heard a rustling noise. Someone was kneeling by his bed, rifling through his saddlebags, and then they moved slowly between the rows of bunks and out the door. Enos slipped out of his covers and followed the man to the Foreman's cabin. He pushed the door open and found Buzzard sitting at his desk. "Working kind of late, ain't you, Pete?"

"Yeah, yeah. I figured I should come back to make sure nobody messes with anything in the camp. What are you doing out in your long johns?"

"I came to get my money."

"You already did. I paid you this afternoon."

"And, then you came into the bunkhouse and stole it."

"That's a lie. I ain't stole nothing. That kind of talk will get you fired."

"You can fire me or not fire me. I don't much care, but I'm giving you two choices. You can give me my money, and we'll pretend this never happened. Shoot, we might even be friends. Or, I can beat you black and blue, take my money, and go someplace that don't have so many thieves. Either way, you ain't keeping my money."

Buzzard reached into his desk and handed Enos two dollars. "I ain't a thief, not really. I got to drinking in town and decided to buck the tiger on the pharaoh table. Lost every cent I had. I just couldn't let the men see me broke, so I did something stupid. You've got no reason to cut me a break, but I'd really appreciate it, if you don't tell the men what I did. It would shame me."

"I thank you for the truth. Now, you've dealt square with me, and I'll do the same for you." He handed him one of his two dollars and said, "I'll see you at breakfast, but don't be late. It might get cold."

* * *

After a long winter with the crudest men he'd ever met, Enos welcomed spring. It was time to plow and time for the new foals, so Enos went home. The ranch had never looked so inviting, as when he viewed it from the crest of a hill. There was someone on the porch. It had to be his mother. He remembered how she liked to shell beans on the porch. Sally and Anna sat on the steps with a bucket between them. His gaze ran to the fields and then the corral. It was so beautiful, so comfortable. How could he have ever left? He spurred his horse down the dirt path and came in at a trot. His mother and sisters didn't run out to meet him. Instead they sat, continuing to toss shelled beans into the bucket, until he dismounted, and his mother said, "Are you home, son?"

"Yes, ma'am. I reckon I had enough of Idaho."

"Well, take your horse out to the barn and brush him down. We'll be having dinner after a while. I'll set a place for you."

Enos was home. Back to the orchards and the cattle and the peaceful ripple of the stream. But it wouldn't take long for the cowboy to rise in his soul again.

* * *

The fall of 1913 found Enos once more camped outside Colfax with Frank Hanna and his horses, waiting for the county fair to open. And, this time Hanna had brought along a new ranch hand, a burly roughneck named Charlie Burton. As the cook handed a plate to Enos, Burton snatched it from his hand. "I reckon he meant to give that plate to me."

"I don't know about that, Charlie, but it looks like to me you're itching for a fight."

"Fight? It wouldn't be much of a fight with you. Yeah, I heard about you, boy. Won yourself a contest last year, everybody's telling you how good you are, and I reckon you figure to win another one this year. Well, you'd better watch your step with me. It's kinda hard to ride them horses with your ribs all busted up and your nose knocked sideways."

Enos was ready to square off, when Frank Hanna stepped in. "All right, that's enough. Lay off the boy, Charlie."

"I ain't done nothing, boss. Just telling him how things are."

Burton walked away, and Hanna wrapped his arm around the young man's shoulders. "Don't let Burton goad you into anything, Enos. I only hired him, because I couldn't find anybody else on short notice. You might want to sleep with one eye open. He ain't the kind to mess with."

"He's a coward. I met lots of his kind at the logging camp. Big talk and no guts. He needs a good lesson."

"Well, you do what you want to do. Just remember, I warned you."

The night passed with no more problems from Burton. Enos rose early the next morning and led a string of horses to the fairgrounds. Some of the spectators were already filtering in, and workers were abuzz, putting everything in place for the rodeo. Enos tied his horses to a picket line and heard a woman's voice, coming from a row of tents. She was loud and bawdy. He thought it was awfully early for someone to be as drunk as she appeared to be. She had her arm wrapped around Charlie Burton's waist. This was too good to be true. He watched them disappear into one of the tents, waited a few minutes, and then mounted one of the horses with his lariat tied to the saddle horn. And, he called out, "Hey, you people over there. Did you come to see a show?" They didn't answer, but he had their attention. He twirled the lasso over his head and said, "Well, watch this." He started at a trot and advanced to a gallop. The rope fell cleanly over a tent post, and Enos yelled at the top of his voice, as the tent flew from its moorings and dragged behind his horse.

Burton and his lover lay nude on a cot. They scrambled to find something to cover themselves, both of them cursing Enos with every breath. But he only laughed and rode in circles until they found another tent to hide in.

Enos knew Burton would be furious, but he didn't run. He sat on his horse and waited for the fight. Burton threw the tent flap open in his bare feet, his clothes a twisted mess. He cursed and bellowed threats, but he never looked up. "Hey, Charlie," Enos said. "If you're looking for your boots, they're behind that green box." Burton sat on the box, pulled his boots on, and Enos called to him again, "Well, big boy, if you've got something to settle with me, I ain't going anywhere. I'm right here, but take a good look. I'm not one of those little guys you been pushing around. Let's do it."

Finally, Burton looked at him, but said nothing. He wagged his head and stormed away. The woman was not so accommodating. She came out of the tent cursing and called Enos names he hadn't heard, even in the logging camp. He pulled his rope free from the tent and spun it around his head. "Now, if you're going to talk like that, I might need to drag you around like I did that tent." With a final curse word and a gesture of her hand, she sprinted into the distance. It had been a long time since Enos had laughed so hard, and he never saw Charlie Burton again.

* * *

Enos scored well at the Whitman County Fair, and it only served to remind him how misplaced he was in the normal, work-a-day world. His mother remarried, which gave him another reason to believe she no longer needed him on the ranch. He spent most of the next year performing in a wild west show, trying to find his place in life, but in 1914 he made his way to his first truly big rodeo. From New York to Los Angeles and Waco to Calgary, people were crazy for rodeos, and there were some good ones, but championships were won at Pendleton.

Dave White nudged his friend in the ribs and said, "Come on, Enos. Pay your money. I've got broncs to bust today."

"Just hold your taters. Don't be in such a hurry to finish second."

"I ain't finishing second today, old son. You'll be watching my dust all day." Enos picked up the receipt for his entry fee and stepped aside, as Dave slapped his money on the table. "Here you go. Just hang onto that for a while. I'll be back later to collect my winnings." He completed his transaction, and the two friends walked toward the arena.

"Well, we've got a couple of hours to kill before the first event. What do you think we ought to do?" Enos asked.

Dave grinned. "I would say we should find some gals who like cowboys, but I wouldn't want them to sap my strength before I win all that money." Then he stopped and said, "Hey, I know an old boy named Ben Corbett. I bet he's got a bottle on him."

"I know Ben. Where do you reckon he is?"

"Down at the stables. He never rents a hotel room, just sleeps in one of the empty stalls."

"All right. Maybe a couple of shots would take the edge off." They passed by a few horse trailers and found Corbett sitting on a bench with a gunny sack at his feet. Enos snatched the hat off Ben's head and dropped it into his lap. "Hey, what are you doing out here on this bench?"

"Just sitting. What does it look like?"

"It looks like you sitting. Time's about up to pay your entry fee, you know."

"You two oil cans don't need to tell me about entry fees. I paid mine an hour ago. Just killing time now."

"Us too. Dave says you might have a drink or two stashed away."

Ben slipped his hat back onto his head and patted the bench. "Have a seat, boys. We Yakima Valley boys need to stick together." They sat, and Corbett drew a bottle from his sack. "Take a swig of this, and you won't remember where the dog bit you."

He was right. By the time they finished the bottle, and half of another, Enos had started to sing. "I wonder who's kissing her now. I wonder who's showing her how. Who's breathing sighs, telling lies."

"Is somebody singing?" Dave asked.
Enos took another drink and said, "Yeah, that would be me."

"Man, you sound like a cow at branding time."

37

"Thank you, and I really mean that."

The three cowboys barely remembered to appear in the arena on time. They leaned against a fence, and Corbett said, "Hey, Dave. They want to know who's gonna ride this next horse."

"What? Oh, I guess I better go." He staggered to the snubbing horse, found his way onto his ride, and said, "Give him to me, and I'll show you gents how we ride these fuzztails over in Yakima." Instead, he showed them how a drunkard rides a horse, and that was to get thrown in the first three seconds.

Ben Corbett laughed his way to his bronc. He almost fell over its back, as he mounted. He managed to say one word, "Yakima", and then he hit the ground.

"Boys, those guys can't hold their liquor," Enos muttered. "They're embarrassing the whole county." He stood erect and marched into the center of the arena. He dug his boots into the stirrups, grabbed the reins, and yelled. "Now you'll see a real Yakima cowboy. Turn this field mouse loose." The bronc spun away with Enos solidly aboard, confident he'd upstage his friends and restore his county's damaged pride. On the third jump, he sailed over the horse's head and landed squarely on his back. "Oh, Mama, that was bad." He managed to get to his feet and brave the derisive laughter until he found Dave and Ben. He wrapped an arm around each of their shoulders, laughed, and said, "Ben, have you got another bottle? I think I need a drink."

Morning came late for Enos and brought with it a pounding head and fragile stomach, capable of holding only a biscuit and some black coffee. He wasn't sure he should even compete, but his fees were paid, and maybe he could redeem himself with a good ride. By noon he was able to eat a slice of pie at the café next to the fairgrounds, but even a BC powder didn't help his headache. He sipped his third cup of coffee, as Frank Hanna sat down. "Have you seen the newspaper today, Enos?"

"I'm not sure I could read the paper if I had one, Frank."

Hanna opened the *Canby Herald*. "Just so you'll know how famous you made yourself yesterday, this ain't the local newspaper. It came in on the train overnight, and the caption is, 'Yakima Canutt leaves the deck of Mrs. Wiggs.' And, they've got a great picture of you leaving that horse." He could scarcely read for laughing. "I don't reckon there's a person in that crowd that don't know where you're from."

"Oh, geez. Here, let me have a look." He pulled the paper across the table, scanned the article, and said, "Well, at least things have got to go up from here. It sure can't get any worse. I can tell you one thing. I'll never take another drink at a rodeo."

When he reached the fairgrounds, he went straight to the judges' box, but they were not there yet. The emcee looked up from his notes and said, "Say, I know you. You're that guy from Yakima."

"Yeah, that's me. Look, I wonder if you'd do me a favor."

"I will if I can."

"I made an idiot of myself yesterday. I'd appreciate it if you'd talk to the competition committee and ask them to give me the toughest horse they have today."

"You want to make up for yesterday?"

"That's right, and I figure I need to do something special. If I can't ride their best horse, then maybe I'm not the cowboy I think I am. But I want to find out."

"It's your funeral, but if you want it that bad, I guess I can get the word to them. The gamblers have already given odds that you won't show up today and, if you do, that you won't last five seconds."

"All the money I have in this world is fifty dollars. But if you see one of those gamblers, tell him I'll bet it all on myself."

It looked like the committee listened. His name was announced, and Enos climbed aboard a tall, thick sorrel, and he made the best ride of his life. At the end, he threw his hat into the air and waved to a cheering crowd. They chanted a new name, "Yakima! Yakima! Yakima!" And, outside his family, the name Enos was heard no more."

* * *

An eight-year-old girl in Los Angeles opened her father's copy of the *Van Nuys Call* and said, "Daddy, what does Yakima mean?"

Claude Rice buttoned the jacket of his police uniform, as he entered the room with his Sunday-morning coffee in hand. "What are you talking about?"

"There's a picture in this newspaper of a man being thrown off a horse, and they call him Yakima."

"Let me see it, Audrea." He held the paper for a few moments, his gaze flowing from top to bottom, and said, "It looks like he's a cowboy, and he comes from the Yakima Valley in Washington. I guess it's a nickname. Judging by the photograph, I'd say he met his match."

"I think he was very brave to ride that dumb, old horse. I've never seen a real cowboy. Will you take me to a rodeo?"

"Well, maybe. Why don't you ask your mother? If she's okay with it, we'll go the next time they come to town."

He kissed her cheek and hurried out the door, as she held the paper to her chest and sighed, "I just love cowboys."

Chapter Three

Even after a winning ride the next day, his drunken display at Pendleton left Yakima with something to prove. On the last day of the rodeo, he asked Dave White for his help. "I think I'm going to try bulldogging. Do you know anybody who can tell me how to do it?"

"No, you don't want to bulldog. That's a good way to get yourself killed."

"I've decided, Dave. I'm going to try it. Can you help me out?"

"Do you see that black man standing over by the grandstand?"

"Yeah. I saw him in the arena yesterday. I mean, I know he can bulldog, but is he the one to show me how?"

White talked as he led Yak toward the man. "That's Bill Pickett, and he was the first man in history to bulldog a steer. I think he can help." They both towered over Pickett, as Dave made the introductions. "Bill, this old boy thinks he wants to bulldog. Could you tell him a thing or two?"

He twisted a piece of rope in his hands and answered. "I can tell you how I do it, but you white boys don't usually ask a colored man like me for help."

Yak couldn't believe his luck. "I don't care about the color of your skin. You're quite a legend, and I'd be proud to learn from you, Mr. Pickett."

"Well, first you need a fast horse. It's a timed event, so you don't need to let your mount cost you any time. But getting there quick ain't the most important thing. You've got to make a clean jump onto the steer. Land on his neck with your arms around his horns, but everybody knows that. What I do is throw my right leg over his left horn. That gets him off balance. Then you kinda let his weight do the work."

"Is it true what they say about you and the lip?"

Pickett twirled the rope with a look of satisfaction. "You bet you, son. If that old bull don't want to go down, I bite his lip as hard as I can. Let him know who's boss."

Yak started to ask another question, but he was interrupted by a female voice. "What he says is true. I've seen him bite steers more than once."

Pickett nodded and said, "Gentlemen, this is the current ladies, world bronc busting champion, Kitty Wilks."

She pointed toward Yak. "What do you smoke, cowboy?"

"Bull Durham."

"Roll me one, will you?"

He took the pouch from his shirt pocket, rolled tobacco into a slip of paper, and licked it shut. He offered her the cigarette and said, "I saw you ride yesterday too. It's pretty plain to see why you're the champion."

"Thank you. What's your name?"

43

"Eno . . ., I mean, Yakima Canutt and this is my friend Dave White."

She struck a match on the sole of her boot and lit her smoke. "Yakima Canutt and Dave White? Can't say that I've heard those names before. Do you boys plan to stay in the rodeo game for long?"

Yak didn't wait for Dave to answer. "I plan to win it all next year."

"Win it all, huh? That's pretty big talk, but if it's true, then you ought to be able to buy me dinner tonight."

"Do you mean just me or me and Dave together?"

"I wasn't talking to Dave."

"Then I'd be glad to, ma'am. How about seven o'clock?" She nodded, and he turned to Pickett. "Could I spend some more time with you talking about bulldogging?"

"Anytime you want. Why don't you take your little gal to dinner and then come see me? I've got a tent set up over by the well."

* * *

Their plates arrived, and Yak watched her dig in like a field hand. "Wow, you must be really hungry."

"Starving. I had two events back-to-back today, so I missed lunch. Oh, I guess you're talking about the way I eat. I grew up with three brothers, and I guess I never learned many manners."

"No, I think you're fine. I was just wondering if you always eat breakfast food for dinner."

"Not always, but I do like a few eggs, over-easy, with peppers and onions. This ain't on the menu, but they make it for me, because, well, I'm a champion, and they like it when I come here."

"You're a famous lady, all right. Everybody in the place is watching you. They're going to watch me like that one day, after I win it all. I'm going to win the Police Gazette belt, Best Overall Cowboy. I guess that sounds big-headed, but it's what I want anyway, and I want it bad."

Kitty spread butter on her toast and said, "I was telling a little bit of a fib today, when I said I never heard of you. I saw you ride."

"They you saw me get thrown."

"I did, and I saw you qualify yesterday. Even with that disaster a couple of days ago, you could still be in the money this week, and that says something. You've got guts, Yakima, and I like that in a man."

"Thank you. Tell me something. You're a pretty girl, not like most of the women in rodeo. You're not big, and you don't walk like a man. Do you know what I mean?"

"You don't have to be a tomboy to ride broncs. I've been telling people that for ten years. You ought to see me when I'm dressed up. It'd knock your eyes out."

"I'd like that. I'd like it a lot. Where do you live, Kitty? Maybe I could come visit you, and we could take one of those picture shows or something."

"Kalispell. It's in Montana, Flathead County. Do you know it?"

"No, but I can find it. But that doesn't sound like a Montana accent."

"That's because I was born and raised in New York."

"A girl who rides like you was born in the city? That's hard to believe." He sipped his coffee and smiled. "I need to know more about you, girl. You're just full of surprises."

"So, uh, when are you going to ask me?"

"Ask you what?"

"About my failed marriage."

"You don't need to tell me about that. Things happen. Some marriages work and some don't. I know that well enough. My parents split up, and I still don't know why."

"Do you mean you don't want to hear a story about him coming home drunk all the time, beating the snot out of me, and running around with other women? About me driving him out the door at the point of a shotgun?" He said nothing. "Well, that's good, because none of that happened. But people always assume it was the woman's fault."

"I don't get into fault, Kitty. I see you for who you are right now, and I like what I see."

* * *

He saw Kitty as often as he could, but mostly at rodeos, and their friendship grew to something more. Yak kept his promise to visit her in Kalispell. They took their seats with a dozen other people in the general store, waiting for the projectionist to finish his preparations for the moving picture. Yak crossed his legs and said, "I didn't know this town was so close to Canada. I reckon you get some cold winters up here."

"Pretty cold, but we're not that much farther north than Washington. I bet you get your share of snow too."

"We do get some snow. So, uh, how the hunting up here?"

"Real good. I shot three deer and a moose last year. We ate good all winter. If you want to come by the house later, I'll fix you a plate of venison." She sat quietly for a moment and then said, "I'm really glad you came, Yak. I wasn't sure you would, but I'm happy you did."

"Me too. I love the countryside, especially that big lake I passed."

"Flathead Lake. It's named for the Flathead Indians, but a lot of stuff around here is named for Indians. It's a good place. You'd like it here."

"I bet I would." Now he sat quietly, wondering if she was hinting at something. "Have you seen a moving picture before?"

"No, but it looks like I'm about to see one now. How about you?"

"Only one. It was called *Across the Plains*, and I saw it in Seattle with my dad. He thought it might be too violent for Mama and my sisters. What's this one called?"

"*The Massacre*. Sounds scary, doesn't it?"

"I reckon so. I guess we need to get quiet, it looks like they're ready." The store owner closed the blinds, and the room fell dark, but for the light at the projector. And, the only sound was the clicking of the reels, as the projectionist turned the hand crank, and the movie began. They watched for half an hour and, at one tense moment in the plot, she took his hand. Yak wasn't sure what he felt for her, but he felt something. The movie ended, and they strolled down the plank walkway of Front Street, just to spend some time together. "That show was something, huh?"

"I felt so bad when Stephen got killed. I mean, he was shielding the girl and her baby with his own body, and the Indians shot him down. And, did you hear that squeal when the bear showed up?"

"Oh, yeah. I thought that lady was going to faint. I guess it's hard not to believe what you see ain't real. I mean, it's real, but it's not really real."
She stopped, wrapped her arms around his neck, and kissed him. "Why don't we get married, Yak?"

"Married? Well, okay. That sounds good to me, but I didn't think it went like this. Am I supposed to tell you I love you?"

"Please don't. My ex-husband told me that, and I don't think I ever want to hear those words from a man again. I like you, Yak, and I believe you like me.

That's enough. I want to marry someone I actually like this time and see how that goes."

"You know, that makes sense to me."

"Then let's do it at a rodeo. There's one coming up to Calgary next month. You go home, tell your friends if you want, and I'll see you then."

* * *

Neither of them was madly in love with the other, but marriage seemed to be the logical next step. The night before the wedding, Dave White and Ben Corbett took Yak bar hopping to celebrate. He had sworn not to drink before an event, but he had not sworn to refuse a drink or two, or ten, with his friends. Dave White poured them all another shot of whiskey and said, "Are you sure about this wedding thing, Yak?"

"I reckon so. It's kind of late for you to be asking that, ain't it? We're tying the knot tomorrow."

"Yeah, I know, and I don't mean any disrespect to your bride, but you know she older than you, don't you? And, this ain't her first time."

"I aim to treat her better than her first husband did. That divorce wasn't her fault. She's a sweet girl. Just wait till you get to know her."

Ben Corbett nudged him in the side and said, "Say, look who just walked in."

Yak turned his fuzzy gaze to a big, powerfully-built man ordering a drink at the other end of the bar. "Oh, I know him. He's that lumberjack I had to throw out of our party last night. I don't think he knew it was a private thing, but he was determined he wasn't leaving. I mean, I think that's him. I ain't seeing so good, but what do I care who drinks here?"

Bill shrugged. "I don't guess you care that he's been talking about you either." He paused to take a drink and then said, "I hear he called you a back-stabber and he called your mother a name I won't repeat."

"He called my mother a name?"

Dave chimed in, "I heard it too. In fact, I was about to fight him over it, but I ain't no match for that big palooka."

Yak downed the rest of his drink and wobbled down the bar. "Hey, you."

The man looked up and said, "Who, me?"

"Yeah, you. I hear you've been talking about me."

"I ain't said nothing about you, friend. You were right to put me out of that party. We've got no issues, as far as I can see."

Yak called his two friends to his side and asked, "Is this the fellow that talked down about my mother?"

They answered in unison, "Yep."

Their word was all the proof he needed, and Yak punched the man squarely in the face. Yak was drunk, and the lumberjack was not. Before he could throw another solid punch, he was on his back with the big man straddling his chest, beating his face bloody. Yak felt powerful hands crushing his throat and he realized this man might actually choke him to death. Then he remembered what his brother had told him so many years ago. He shifted his weight to one side and freed his arm enough to jab his thumb into the man's eye. In a matter of seconds, the fight was over, and the lumberjack was stumbling out the door yelling, "That ain't fair."

"Yeah, well there's no such thing as a fair fight."

Dave helped him to his feet and said, "Look, that fella that just beat the snot out of you, well, he never called you anything. Me and Ben made that up. We thought it'd be funny to see you in a fight before you get married."

Yak wasn't so drunk that he couldn't knock both of his friends onto their backsides. Then he pulled them up and said, "Come on, boys. Help me get back to the hotel. I'm getting married tomorrow, you know."

* * *

Another morning and another headache, but Yakima couldn't let this one keep him from the woman he was about to marry. Two black eyes stared back at him from the mirror. The cuts and bruises on his face made shaving a chore. He wasn't sure how clearly he might say the "I do's" with his lips swollen double their normal size. Breakfast was oatmeal with sips of milk. Was he missing a tooth? No, maybe not. But when two o'clock arrived, he stood at the side entrance to the church, his best friends beside him and every joint aching liked he'd been trampled by a mule. Dave straightened his tie and said, "Boy, you are a mess, son. Would you like a drink before you go in?"

Yak knew he shouldn't, but his body told him he should. "Have you got some?" White took a pint from his back pocket, and Yak carefully downed half the bottle. "Oh, yeah, the hair of the dog. Help me in there, boys. I'm ready to meet my bride." They followed him inside, and he stood before the altar.

The minister smiled and said, "It looks like you slept in those clothes."

"No sir, but I did sleep *on* them. Guess I didn't see them laying on the bed." Then the organ played, and Kitty came down the aisle. Yak thought she looked like an angel, beautiful and innocent. When she got close, her sweet expression fell, she sniffed the air near him, and her eyes turned from angelic to a fiery glare. But, she took his hand as they exchanged vows, and he felt better. He'd make it up to her. After all, he had to defend his name. She'll understand.

The wedding went smoothly, and the small reception after found Kitty with her arms wrapped around him as often as she could. Laughter filled the room, especially when Yak tried to dance with her. And, just after eleven, they crossed the street to their hotel room. He latched the door, loosened his tie, and took her in his arms. But she pulled away. "What's the matter, baby?"

"What's the matter? You showed up for my wedding smelling like a brewery, your face beaten black and blue, and you want to know what's the matter?"

"Look, I know I messed up. I went out to celebrate with Dave and Ben last night, you know, 'cause I was going to marry you. We were having a good time, having a few, and I thought this guy had been talking about me. As it turns out, he hadn't, but I didn't know that. So, well, it ain't as bad as it looks."

"You drunken fool. I can tell you this much. This might be our wedding night, but you won't be riding this filly, and maybe not for a long time."

And, now he saw the other side of his angel. "Suit yourself. I'll be at the bar." The night drew long, and the bourbon did little to soothe his pain. He'd been hurt many times, broken bones and long, ragged gashes, but this was very different. And, the more he thought about it, the more he understood how stupid it was to ruin the wedding with his boyish antics.

"People like me ought not be allowed to drink," he mumbled.

"What's that, sir?" the bartender asked. "Did you want another?"

"No, I've had more than enough. I think I'll go to bed." He reached the room, expecting another tongue lashing, but he found Kitty fast sleep. He dropped his clothes and eased into bed beside her. And, when he woke she was standing at the door, fully dressed and smiling.

"I'm going down to have some breakfast, sweetheart. Why don't you get dressed and meet me in the restaurant?"

"Uh, okay." What happened to the banshee that blessed him out last night? It took but a few minutes for him to wash his face, don a fresh shirt and jeans, and work his way down the stairs. She motioned for him to sit beside her and asked the waiter to fill his cup with coffee. Yak wasn't quite sure what to make of this, but he sipped the strong brew and collected his thoughts. "I want to tell you how sorry I am about what happened. It was all my fault, and you had a right to be mad at me. It was a dumb thing to do, and I promise you I won't do that again."

"You're still a wild, young buck, aren't you? That's part of what drew me to you, but you've got to get hold of that part of who you are. I've been on the rodeo circuit for ten years, and I've never seen a more talented bronc buster than you, but you're doing your best to throw it away. Look around you, Yak. Most of the men in rodeo are bums. Yes, they can ride and bulldog, but what else can they do? What's going to become of them by the time they're fifty? They'll be begging in the streets, that's what, if they ain't dead."

"I don't think it's that bad. Some of those guys are friends of mine."

"What kind of friends get you drunk and ruin your wedding day? If you want to be with me, you need to get rid of those guys. I can make you a champion."

He took another drink of coffee, thought about the things she'd said, and answered. "I don't need you to be a champion. I can do that all by myself, and I won't turn my back on friends who were with me in the tough times, when I needed them. No, I ain't that kind of man."

"Then you're not the kind of man I can build a life with." It was a difficult start to their time together, and a sign of things to come.

* * *

Within a year, Yakima was winning as many bulldogging events as he was bronc busting, and that was a lot. At twenty-one he returned to Pendleton and qualified for the finals in bronc riding. He threw his saddle over a brute of an animal named Cul de Sac, the horse he drew for his ride. This was a bronc he could win on, but it was also one that could throw him with his first buck. Dave White stood beside him with his hand on the snubbing horse. "Well, it looks like they picked the right cowboys, Yak. It's you, me, and Bob Hall."

"Yeah, I'm glad you made it, but we're both going to have to do some big-time riding to beat Bob. He's first class and, to tell you the truth, I'm a little nervous."

"Uh, did you see the squaw race? The crowd went crazy for it."

"I appreciate what you're doing, Dave, but you don't have to try and get my mind off it. Once I hit the saddle, I'll be all right."

"Ain't you cinching that saddle a little loose? This boy'll kick your butt, if you ain't locked in tight."

"I'll take that chance. If I cinch him too tight, he might not buck good, and I need everything he's got to win. There's no looking back for me. I'm gonna do all I can to win this thing. I have to."

"This ain't about Kitty, is it? I know you guys have had it rough."

"She's gone, moved out, and filed for divorce. I guess that's it, but it's hard to get my head right. I thought about joining the Army or something, just to get away for a while. But this ain't about her. It's about me and this old horse here. I ain't looking back and, for once in my life, I'm not going to second guess myself. I'm going all out, win or bust."

"Well, good luck to you, Yak. I'm up next, so try not to tear the fence down, will you?"
He walked away, and Yak stepped onboard with the reins in his left hand and his hat in his right. "Let me have him."

The Olympics of the West had reached its premiere event, and Yakima Canutt was center stage. Cul de Sac pulled away in a spin and began to bawl, as he kicked and jumped. He whirled fast and crooked, but Yak held on and worked his spurs from shoulders to cantle. A mighty back kick lifted him off the saddle. He wondered if he should ease off his spurs for a jump to settle back down, but this was no time to be careful. The bronc landed hard and reversed, and finally he ran out of tricks. He calmed to a trot, and Yak threw his Stetson into the air. He leapt to the ground, waving to the crowd, and found a seat next to the grandstands. His part was over. All he could do now was watch and wait.

Dave White rode P.J. Nutt to a finish and then sat beside Yak. "That was a good ride, Dave." "Thanks, but I don't think it was enough. The only guy you've got to worry about is Bob, and he's got Angle. You know, Lew Minor won a championship on that horse."

"Yes, I know. You're not making me feel any better about this." They watched as Hall mounted and made a fantastic ride. When it was over, he walked by Yak and Dave with a shrug. "Yeah, that's kind of how I feel too, Dave. I don't think you could wedge a dime between our two rides."

"Congratulations, Yak, I think you've got him sacked."

"I hope so, but we won't know that till the man in the crow's nest says so."

Time crept by, as the judges conferred and seemed to argue. And then, the head judge raised his megaphone. "In the cowboy's saddle bronc riding for the World Championship . . ." A pregnant pause covered the arena before he said, "Yakima Canutt first, Bob Hall second, and Dave White third." It was everything Yak ever wanted to achieve, or so he thought. He had money in his pocket, and his name was noted in the newspapers as a champion, not a drunken joke. But he wanted more championships. He

57

had to prove this was not just a fluke. He would be the best ever or break his neck trying.

* * *

Yakima Canutt was the best cowboy in America, but his marriage was not the best. He and Kitty avoided each other, one competing in Waco while the other went to Calgary. Even when they were in the same town, they seldom saw each other. The loneliness and distance between them weighed heavily on Yak. He tried to mend their relationship, but nothing worked. Then the Great War arrived, and he enlisted in the Navy. Each day began with a light breakfast and a three-mile run. After three weeks of boot camp, he reported to the rifle range with his chief, Harold Crosby. "All right, Canutt, put as many slugs as you can somewhere close to the center of that target. And, try not to miss the whole thing."

The rifle fell against his shoulder like an old friend. "I'll do my best not to embarrass you, Chief." He fired, reloaded, and fired again eight times, all inside the inner circle. Then he dropped to one knee, and sent another eight shots just as good. "Did you want me to lay down and shoot?"

"Be careful with that smart mouth of yours, seaman, or you'll be shining garbage cans."

"Yes, sir. I'm working on that, but it don't come natural."

"That's good shooting, Canutt, but you know that. The problem is that you make an awfully big target. I

58

guess that's why you enlisted in the Navy instead of the infantry."

"I just wanted to see the world and help with the war effort. I figured this was a good place to do that."

"To me, you're one in a long line of sailors I see every year, but to the Navy you're that famous rodeo cowboy. They won't be sending you to war, son. You're too valuable at helping recruit other guys to join. You'll be put on exhibition."

"That's not what I signed up for."

"The Navy isn't worried about what you signed up for. It's interested in what you can do to help. Now, we don't have any bulls to wrestle, but we do have a boxing team. Do you think you want to be part of that?"

"Boxing? I always liked a good fight. Sure, why not?"

"I'll take you over to the gym when we finish here and get you signed up. We've got a couple of matches set for tonight. I'll set you up with someone, and we'll see what you've got."

* * *

Yakima stood in line with nine other sailors, waiting to see who he'd face in his first bout. At six-four, he was as big as anyone in the locker room. Crosby walked down the line, and the first fighter he chose was Yak. "Now, let me see who'd be a good opponent for this big boy. Yeah, you, Foster."

"Who?" Yak asked. "Come on, Chief, you can't be serious. He's half my weight. I'd beat him to death."

Tall and wiry, the young sailor paled next Yak's 194 pounds. He grinned and said, "What's wrong, cowboy? Are you scared?"

"Yeah, I'm scared. Scared of the wrath of God, scared of grizzly bears, and I'm scared I'll put you in the morgue. But, if you've got to have it that way, let's go." They walked from the locker room into the gym, to a boxing ring surrounded by dozens of sailors. The men began to chant Foster's name, and Yak thought, "These guys are crazy."

The bell rang for the first of three rounds, and Yak came out with a sweeping punch, but Foster sidestepped it. He stung Yak's face with a left jab, circled, and jabbed him again. Every time Yak tried to throw a punch, Foster punished him with hooks and crosses, then danced away. The pattern was unbroken for two rounds, and Yak knew he was losing badly. He had to do something. In the third, he grabbed Foster and whispered profanities. But his insults changed nothing. At the end of the round, the referee ruled the match a draw and called them back to the center of the ring for a fourth round. He looked at Yak and said, "I heard what you said, and I decided to let this boy beat on you some more." And, he did.

When it was over, they shook hands, and Yak said, "You'd never beat me in a real fight."

"This was a real fight, or weren't you paying attention."

"I'm talking about a rough-and-tumble. The kind of fight that tells you who the man is."

"I'll fight you anytime and anywhere. You name it."

"Ten o'clock tomorrow morning at the west gate. There's a patch of woods down there."

"Done."

* * *

His face was still aching when Yak reached the west gate the next morning. He brought a friend, and Foster brought three. "What's the deal, Foster? Did you bring reinforcements?"

"Don't worry about those guys. They're here to see me whip you and watch you get on your knees to take back that name you called me."

They reached a clearing in the trees, and the onlookers formed a small circle around them. Yakima cracked his knuckles and said, "Okay, now this is bare-fist with no rules except no kicking and biting."

"You don't need to have exceptions for me, but get ready to eat a lot of pudding. When I'm finished, you'll have to gum your dinner."

The fight started as the last one had ended, with Foster landing quick punches, but he had little room to dance. Yak grabbed him around the waist, hoisted him up, and slammed him to the ground. As he rose, he hit him and then backed off. Foster stood and threw a few more jabs, before Yak caught him again and took him down with both knees in his chest. Three hard blows to the face, and Yak stopped. "Have you had enough?" Foster shook his head, and Yak punched him again. Finally, Foster gave in. "Okay, I give up. Don't hit me anymore."

Yak stood and helped him to his feet. "You're all man, Foster, and you sure know how to take a punch. I apologize to you for what I called you. It was a stupid thing to say."

"It takes a big man to say that, cowboy. Let's forget about it." As time went on, they became close friends. Foster taught Yak how to move in the ring, and Yak taught him to shoot. When boot camp ended, they parted, never to see each other again.

* * *

The crowd at Pendleton packed the arena, cheering the good rides and booing the lesser ones. One of the security people approached Yak and said, "Sorry, sailor, but you can't be out here. Competitors only."

"I am a competitor. Didn't you see me bulldogging this morning?"

The guard studied him for a moment. "Wait a minute, you're that guy from the Yakima Valley. Canutt, ain't it?"

"That's right. The Navy gave me a thirty-day leave to defend my championship."

"I saw you win this morning, and I couldn't figure out why you were in uniform."

"Publicity stunt. The event organizers thought the crowd would like it."

"Didn't you get hurt in the bulldogging? I was watching when that bull rammed you into the fence."

"He banged me up pretty good. The doc wrapped my ribs up real tight, and here I am. Say, have you got any chew on you?" The man handed him a pouch, and Yak pressed a wad of tobacco into his jaw. "I always like a good chew when I ride. Well, I'd better go. I've got old Monkey Wrench today. Wish me luck."

"Yeah, you'll need some on that nag."

Only a few months had passed since he last rode a bronc, but climbing the chute fence felt strange, until he settled into the saddle. And, then he was home. He adjusted the reins and nodded for the gate to open. Monkey Wrench came out like a champion, jumping high and kicking at the sky. He made a quick twist, and that loosened Yak in the saddle, but he hung on, holding the stirrups with his toes. Then the horse ducked his head and threw his rider off end over end. Yak hit the dirt more humiliated than hurt, but still he was hurt. His ribs barked at him, and there was something more. It felt like a sponge sapping his strength and robbing him of his breath. He waved to the crowd, as he hobbled out of the arena, but he couldn't deny that something was very wrong.

The train ride back to his camp at Bremerton included a cuspidor by his side, not for tobacco spit, but for his spells of nausea. The odor kept anyone from sitting with him, and that was fine with Yak. He propped his feet on the opposing seat and slept until the conductor called his station. When he reached the Navy base, they sent him straight to the doctor. "Influenza," he said.

"I don't know exactly what that is, doctor, but I sure feel like I'm dying."

"And, you may be. We don't know as much as we'd like to know about it yet, and we have no real treatment for it. You'll have to be placed in isolation to keep the disease from spreading to other people."

"How long will I be in the hospital?"

"I'm afraid the hospitals are full. This influenza epidemic has spread all over the base and all over town. The hospitals are packed with sick people. You'll be assigned a cot in the armory."

"Then what?"

"You'll have to tough it out the best you can. It's all in God's hands now."

* * *

Yakima's cot stood near the east wall of the armory, among nearly two hundred others. A young woman looked down on him, her cap and mask obscuring everything but her blue eyes. "You're going to be here for a while, Mr. Canutt. If you need anything, like maybe water, let me know, and I'll try to get it for you."

"Thank you, nurse."

"Oh, I'm not a nurse. I'm just a volunteer. The nurses are all at the hospitals. My name is Kristin."

"Well, then, thank you, Kristin. Who are these guys beside me?"

"On your left is Seaman Caruthers, and . . ."

The sailor to his right spoke up, "George Willingham. I got here about an hour ago, but Caruthers over there, well, I don't know about him. He looks really sick to me."

Kristin touched Yak's shoulder with her gloved hand and said, "Okay, I'll be around for the next ten hours."

She walked away, and Willingham propped himself up on one elbow. "I tried to tell them I don't need to be here. I've just got a cold. Anyway, did you bring any cards? Maybe we could play some poker till they let us out of here."

"Sorry, George, but I didn't bring a thing. The doc was afraid I'd infect somebody, so he sent me straight here from his office. I don't even have a toothbrush."

"I'll see if that Kristin will bring us some cards, when she comes back around. I need something to do besides just lay here."

Yak mumbled a few words even he didn't understand before he fell to sleep. His high fever kept him delusional much of the time. He dreamed of days long gone, planting time on the ranch, the times his grandfather told him stories of crossing the plains, and the horses he had ridden. Then there were the nightmares, indescribable creatures that tormented him, and he too weak to fight back. In those rare times when he found peaceful sleep, someone would start crying, or a gurney would rattle down the aisle with another sailor being taken away in a basket. The taste of blood filled his mouth from a throat too ravaged for him to talk beyond a whisper, and his pillow bore witness to the overflow that crept from the corners of his mouth. At times he wished he would die, but he remembered the doctor's words. He was in God's hands and, surely, He was not finished with him yet.

Yak woke the next morning to find a deck of cards laying on the floor next to his cot. He looked over to George Willingham, but his pillow bore the same red stains as his own, and his face was the color of ash. Caruthers was gone. Another sailor lay asleep in his place. "Hey, George," he whispered. "What happened to him?"

Willingham's voice was as weak as his own. "Died during the night. I don't know the new guy." He picked up the deck of cards and asked, "Do you want to play a game?" But, when he tried to shuffle, the cards fell across his blanket.

"That's okay, George. I didn't want to play anyhow." Kristin came around with a sip of water for his parched throat and a wet cloth for his head. It felt like God's own mercy, the cool water trickling down the side of his face and into his ear. Every word he said burned, but he found the strength to say, "When George and I get out of here, we're going to play the best game of poker, and I'm going to take all his money."

She smiled and answered, "You do that, sailor, and I'll help you spend it." When her shift ended, Kristin did not go home. She stayed through the night, tending to Yak and the others, wiping feverish heads and holding weak hands of those about to die.

Hers was the first face he saw, when Yak awoke the next morning. "Thank you for staying with me."

"Well, it was a critical time, so I didn't want to leave you, but your fever broke during the night. I think you're going to be okay."

"What about George? Did his fever break?"

"I'm afraid we lost him."

"Oh, God, no. I live, and he dies. How can you figure it?"

"I've been here for several weeks watching people die. I don't try to figure it."

"No, I guess not. I'm just happy to be alive." By the end of the week, Yak was eating soup and regaining his strength. He'd watched dozens of young men die in those few days, but it wasn't his turn, not yet. Two days later, he was discharged, and he asked the head nurse, "Can you tell me how to get in touch with Kristin?"

"I don't know anyone named Kristin."

"She's the volunteer who took care of me. I just want to let her know how much I appreciate her help. Without her, I don't think I would've made it."

"We have no one by that name."

"Sure, you do. Young woman, blue eyes."

"Mr. Canutt, I hired every person in this armory, including all the volunteers. Trust me, there is no Kristin."

"But . . ."

"No, sailor. Now, take your belongings and go. Oh, here. This telegram came for you while you were sick." He tore it open and read, "Heard you won money in Pendleton. Don't forget your alimony. Kitty."

* * *

When he returned to his unit, Captain Walden called him to his office. "Sit down, Canutt. I'm glad to see you survived your illness. A lot of our boys didn't. The whole town has been devastated."

"Thank you, sir. I'm glad to be here." Yak sat in a wooden chair, his Navy cap in his hands. "Before we get too far, I want to thank you again for letting me ride at Pendleton."

"Yeah, I heard about that. What made you think it was a good idea to ride in your uniform? Don't you have any more respect for the United States Navy than to rodeo in your whites?"

"Oh, well, the promoters thought it would, you know, add some color for the fans. I guess maybe it wasn't such a good idea."

"It was a long, long way from a good idea, but we'll talk about that when you get back from France."

"When am I going to France, sir?"

"You and the horses you broke for the French Army sail in three days. The French have a tough time talking with their troops in the field. Radio communications are spotty at best. The often rely on foot messengers running from one location to another. You are going to teach those messengers to ride, and to ride well."

Yakima could not hold back the grin that spread over his face. "Horses? The horses I trained? Yes, sir. I'll teach them right. By the time I finish, they'll ride forward and backward."

"Just teach them to ride. And, you should know that our French allies don't always welcome our help. Even the ones that speak English might pretend they don't just to make your job harder."

"Why would they do that? We're on the same side. I don't understand that."

"And, you never will. Who can understand the French?"

Yak packed and made it to the ship three hours early. He stowed his gear and went directly to the hold, where the horses stood in makeshift stalls with hay strewn across the metal floor. He walked from one horse to the next, stroking their heads and calling their names, until he reached his favorite, Tumbleweed. He whispered to her. "There you are, girl. Hey, don't tell the rest, but you're the best of the lot. There ain't a horse here that holds a candle to you. Don't tell the French, but I might sneak you back home with me." She nudged him as if she understood what he was saying. Tumbleweed had a spirit like none of the others, and Yak had missed her.

When they reached the French coast, they were transported to a camp outside the village of Braine. The next morning Yak walked down a picket line where the horses were tied and met with Captain Lucere and his troop of messengers. "Good morning, Captain."

"Bon jour. What shall I call you, a sailor or a cowboy?"

"Just call me Yak."

"Yak? Tell me, Yak, are you a cowboy from Oklahoma?"

"Washington, but I went to Oklahoma once. I remember it was hot there, but nobody knew how hot it was."

"They did not know? Have you no thermometers in America?"

"Oh, yeah. They said it was a hundred degrees in the shade, but I couldn't find any shade." He waited for a laugh and got none. "Okay, then. Is everybody ready to start?"

"Qui, but I must tell you. My men already know how to ride. To be quite honest with you, monsieur, I don't understand why you are here. My men and I find it insulting."

"Yeah, I thought you might. Well, before you send me home, can we have a little fun together?"

"Fun? How do you mean?"

"There's an orchard just behind that tent over there. Have a one of your men go pick, oh say, half a dozen apples and put them on the posts of that fence."

70

Lucere looked confused, but his men collected the apples and placed them on posts about ten feet apart. Yak led Tumbleweed from the picket line, stopped her fifty feet from the first post, and walked back to the captain. "One more thing. Would you loan me your pistol?"

"My pistol?"

Yak nodded, and Lucere handed it over. "All right, now, Captain, everybody best stand back. You say these boys know how to ride. Well, I'm going to show you what they don't know. We'll start with the Crupper mount." He stuffed the revolver into his waistband, ran toward Tumbleweed, and leapfrogged over her rump into the saddle. He turned her in a circle, drew her onto her hind legs, and then charged down the fence line. As he approached each post, he shot the apple to bits. When he reached the end, he threw his right foot over the saddle and bounced off the ground from one side of the horse to the other. They sped past Lucere at a full gallop for another twenty yards. Then Yak stood on the saddle and rode back.

Lucere's mouth stood agape. "Forgive me, monsieur. I see we have things to learn."

"Thank you, Captain. Now, I ain't gonna teach your guys all that, but it might come in handy if they learn to ride on one side of the horse, so maybe they don't get shot so easy. But mostly they need to learn to ride fast over rugged ground." He spent the rest of the day teaching basic riding skills, and his students appeared eager to learn.

When the day was over, Lucere came back. "You have done a good day's work with my men, and I would like to show my appreciation. There is a family that lives a few kilometers from here. We pay them to provide meals to our officers, and I hope you will allow me to take you there for dinner."

"That sounds good to me."

"Before the war, they had a vineyard. It's gone now, but their cellar is still well provided with wine."

"Wine? I gave up hard liquor, but I don't suppose a little wine would hurt." Yak rode in Lucere's car to a farmhouse, dined on rabbit and asparagus, and then accepted the family's offer to spend the night. He rose the next morning thinking that, with food and hospitality like this, maybe war wasn't such a bad thing. When he reached the camp, he learned it was very bad. The field was littered with the remains of dead horses, every one of them laying on its side. "My God, Captain, what happened?"

"Mustard gas. The Germans attacked the camp while we were gone. Twenty-six men dead. Their bodies were moved for preparation to bury."

Yak wandered through the field, aghast at the sight of such destruction. He found Tumbleweed, knelt beside her, and let his tears fall onto her brown coat.

"Are you weeping for the horses and not the men?" Lucere asked.

"I mean no disrespect to the soldiers. Mustard gas is a cowardly way to fight, but your men are like me. We knew what we were doing when we joined up. We came to kill Germans, but the Germans killed them. Horses have no politics. They were just being horses."

Chapter Four

When the war ended, he came home, leaving the bottle behind him. He was fully grown, hardened by warfare, and a divorced man, hungry to prove himself again. And, what he knew best was rodeo.

Yak travelled to Los Angles to ride a horse name Poncho Villa. Douglas Fairbanks doubled the prize money to $500. Yak took his money and made a new friend. He wintered in LA, where some of his old rodeo pals, like Ben Corbett and Tom Mix, had started working in the movie business. Mix invited him to appear in a couple of his movies, and Yak began to develop a taste for Hollywood. But there was another taste in his mouth, and it came to the front with the arrival of a special-delivery letter. "Hey, Ben, do you know a guy named Charley Wilson?"

"Yeah. He's a rich guy. I mean really rich. He owns a bunch of horses, but the best of the bunch is Tipperary."

"Tipperary? I never heard of Charley Wilson, but I sure know who Tipperary is. He's the horse that never been rode."

"I hear he's thrown over eighty cowboys. Nobody's come close to riding him."

"Well, this letter says Mr. Wilson wants me to try it up in Belle Fourche on the Fourth of July. He's offering me $500, if I can ride Tipperary till he stops bucking."

"Do you have to ride by competition rules?"

"Uh, let me see. Yeah." He pointed to a line in the letter. "Look at that. He says, 'Come up and try to ride him.' He's daring me."

"I'd let that go, if I was you, Yak, don't' let some rich guy push you into this. Those cowboys that horse threw weren't just a bunch of bums. They were circuit riders, some of them champion caliber. He threw Curly Roberts and Earl Thode. You've got nothing to win in that deal."

"Well, there's five hundred bucks to win."

Corbett took the letter and scanned through it. "Look, it ain't worth it. Why do you think these Hollywood people are inviting you to be in movies? I'll tell you why. You're a rodeo champion, probably the best to ever ride the circuit, a dadgum hero. I was never half the rider you are, and I'm still making real good money in these movies. Man, you could get rich at it. If you go up there and let this Tipperary embarrass you, those offers might just disappear."

Yakima did not hesitate. "What kind of odds do you think you could get on some bets?"

"Did you hear a word I said?"

"Odds, Ben, odds."

"All right. The people in Montana know you, so the odds won't be as high as somebody like me trying to ride him, but I'd say two to one, maybe two and a half."

"Good. I've still got most of the money I made in *Lightning Bryce*. You go up a couple of days early and place some bets for me. I'll give you a piece of what I win."

"And, what if you don't win?"

"Then I might need to borrow train fair to get home, so don't spend all your money."

* * *

Charley Wilson straightened his bolo tie, as he crossed the arena to where Yakima stood checking his gear for his upcoming ride on Tipperary. "How are you feeling, Yak?"

"Good, Mr. Wilson, good. It looks like we're gonna have a big crowd."

"Yeah, this kind of side act is good for the rodeo. It's something different for people to talk about, and it gives them another place to place bets. That's why I came to see you."

"Do you want to make a wager on the ride? I'll have to check with Ben to see how much money I have left."

"No, it isn't that. The truth is I'm a little worried. There's a couple of rough-looking guys asking around about you. I think they might be with the mob." He glanced over Yak's shoulder and said, "Here they come now. I'd better go, but you be careful. Their kind doesn't play around."

Yak took the knife from his pocket, knelt by his bag, and eased his pistol onto one leg. He whittled notches in the handle, pulled his shirt tail loose, and shoved the gun into his waist band. He stood as they arrived, and the shorter man spoke. "Are you Canutt?"

"Yep, and who are you?"

"Our names don't matter. We're here to talk business."

"Okay, but I don't have much time. What do you have in mind?"

"We represent investors in Chicago who have a certain interest in your ride today. A lot of people say you're going to ride Tipperary, and our bosses bet a ton of money that you won't"

"Well, I'm afraid your bosses stand to lose a lot of money then."

"We don't think so. You could get rich quick, if you play it smart. It's easy money."

"Do you mean like Jack Johnson? Yeah, I saw the film clips of his fight with Jess Willard in Cuba. And, I saw the picture of him lying on the canvas with a big grin on his face. They call it the hundred-thousand-dollar grin."

"We wouldn't know anything about that."

"Everybody knows he took a dive in that fight. He even admitted it."

"Are you looking to make a hundred grand, too, cowboy?"

"Not from you. I'll make my money from the bets I placed, and my bets say I'll ride Tipperary to a stop. I don't sell out, not to you, not to anybody." The bigger man slipped his hand under his coat, and Yak pulled his shirttail up. "Don't do something you'll regret, big boy. Take a close look at the grip on that pistol. There's five notches, and I've got room for a couple more."

The men said nothing more. As they walked away, Charley Wilson returned. "Was that what I thought it would be?"

"They offered to pay me to throw this ride today."

"What did you say?"

"I told them no, so they kind of threatened me, but I've been threatened before."

"Yak, I hope you don't think I sent those guys to you. I'm betting my horse will throw you in the first minute, but I don't associate with bums like that."

"Mr. Wilson, that thought never came into my mind, and I'll prove it to you. We have three judges today. You get to pick one, the competition committee picks one, and I pick one. Well, I'm picking you."

"That's going too far, son. You don't know me that well."

"I know you well enough. If you had been in with those guys, you wouldn't have warned me they were coming. In fact, it's already done. You are my judge."

"I don't know what to say."

"Don't say anything. Just call the ride as you see it."

* * *

The bets had been placed, the judges selected, and all that was left was for America's champion to try his luck on the horse that couldn't be ridden. Yak stood by the snubbing horse with Ben Corbett beside him, admiring the bronc he had come to ride. "Look at him, Ben. He's a thoroughbred, you know."

"And, he looks it. I've never seen a more beautiful animal."

"I read up on him. Mr. Wilson bought him from the Army. They thought he wasn't good enough because he wasn't a pacer, and now look at him. If they gave a trophy to horses, he'd win it. He's looking right through me, like he's gonna chew me up and spit me out. Yeah, he's a proud one. He's got the right to be proud." Yak moved closer, took the harness in his hands, and whispered in the horse's ear. "Oh, son, you're going to meet your match today. I already love you, and there ain't no man got the right to break your spirit, including me, but only one of us can win. So, don't get your feelings hurt and be mad at me. This is the day you get rode."

"Yak, are you talking to that horse?"

"Yep, and he's talking to me. Now, step aside, Ben. Me and this old boy have got some business to settle." Yak eased into the saddle, took the reins, and said, "Let me have him." Tipperary burst into the arena like a cyclone. He whirled and kicked, snorting more like a bull than a horse. Yak had never been on a ride like this. Every bounce felt like it broke another part of his back. It was like riding Satan himself, a fiery demon of an animal. When he finally worked his rider loose in the saddle, Tipperary turned his head. Those eyes that had looked through Yak moments ago dared him to stay aboard. Told him he would be the next to fall. Yak pressed his boots deeper into the stirrups, yanked on the reins, and said, "Not today!" The harder he fought, the harder Tipperary bucked, until he gave out. And, with a final snort, he settled into a trot.

Yak dismounted, and the first man to greet him was Charley Wilson. "That was something, Yak."

"Thank you, sir, and thank you for letting me ride him. You were right about Tipperary. He's is the best there is."

"Well, you got the best of him today, but I bet you can't ride him again."

"Rub him down, give him some rest, and I'll ride him again tomorrow."

"Uh, no, I don't think so. I'm going to take him home. But, when the time is right, you can give him another go, and I'll wager three to one he throws you."

"A thousand dollars, Mr. Wilson?"

"You're on, Mr. Canutt." Yak didn't know if he'd ever match the feeling he had when he stepped down from Tipperary. It was the most challenging and most thrilling thing he'd ever done. And, in the spring of the next year, he took Charley Wilson's money.

* * *

Over the next five years, Yakima Canutt won three more championships, the Roosevelt Award, and more rodeo events that he could count. He had become a household name across America, and the Canadians said he owned the Calgary Stampede. He also bore the pain of lingering injuries and torn ligaments he earned along the way. On his first trip to Texas, he won big in Fort Worth and then he received a telegram that read, *Meet me at the Alamo – Paul Hurst.*

The rodeo in San Antonio was not scheduled to start for another four weeks, but Yak went early, and he met Hurst next to the barracks. "Why did you want to meet here?" he asked.

"I thought it would be easy to find, since you haven't been here before. Anybody in the city can tell you how to get to the Alamo."

"Well, I've heard about it, but it's a lot smaller than I expected."

"Yeah, we only have this building and the church left, and the Quartermaster turned it into storage during the war. They're supposed to install a concrete roof on the mission soon. Most people seem disappointed when they first see it. But Texans still love it."

"So, what's this about?"

"We're shooting a movie, and we need a couple of men who can ride and do stunts. We'll shoot part of the movie here and some scenes across the border.

Oh, and we'd want you to help us with publicity."

"I ain't much of a talker, Paul."

"You don't need to be. We'd stage a bronc busting event in the streets of Houston, you know, get some newspaper and radio people there. It pays five hundred a week, and we'd need you for at least a month."

"It sounds okay. I've got to fill the time somehow, but there is one condition. Once the rodeo starts, I'll need a few days off to compete in that. After all, I'm a rodeo cowboy, not a movie star."

"Done. We're staying at the Hot Wells Hotel. It's well out of town and has some dirt roads around it, so it'll be great for working your horses and keeping in shape."

Yakima laughed and said, "Little Enos Canutt in a movie. Mama will never believe it.

* * *

The movie company shot their scenes in San Antonio and moved to Nuevo Laredo, Mexico. The old jail and shabby streets offered an ideal setting for a western, but Hurst seemed to be having a problem with the head jailer. He turned away, clearly frustrated, and said, "That makes no sense."

"What's wrong, Paul?" Yak asked.

"I asked him if we could shoot inside the jail, and he says it's against the rules. What rules?"

"Let me talk to him." Yak walked past Hurst and noticed the Masonic pin on the jailer's shirt. As he shook his hand, he gave the sign only Masons understand. "Are you a travelling man?

"Ah, yes, senor. And, I see that you are."

"Look, these boys would like to film a few scenes inside, and I'm not asking you to break any rules, but is there some way you could let them in, just for a few minutes?"

"How are you connected to this company?"

"Hired help. They pay me by the week. I've got no money at stake in this."

"I will let you do this filming, if you will join me for a drink tonight."

"Well, yeah, sure. Where?"

"There is a very nice cantina at the edge of town, Rosita's. Eight o'clock?"

Yak nodded and walked back to Hurst. "Okay, he'll let you in, but you need to be out of there in half an hour. And, I think it would be a good idea if you meet him and me at the cantina tonight."

"I thought you gave up alcohol."

"I'm trying, but it seems like every time I swear off the sauce, somebody want to buy me a drink."

* * *

The sound of guitars and castanets echoed off the adobe walls of Rosita's cantina, as three men sat in a corner, quietly talking. Hurst ran a finger around the rim of his glass and said, "It was very thoughtful of you to let us film in your building today, and we'd like to show our appreciation. If you have a charity you support, we'll make a donation."

"That is very kind." He glanced over Hurt's shoulder and said, "My apologies for what is about to happen." A young woman in a colorful dress strode to their table and laid her hand on the back of Yakima's neck. "You are Americans, no?"

Yak had seen this come-on before. "Yes, ma'am, we are. And, what is your name?"

"I am Astoria, and I am here to help you have a good time while you are in Mexico. What can I do to make you happy? I can get you anything."

Yak stood, took hold of her arm, and led her to the bartender. "Look, buddy, we just came to have a couple of drinks. Don't you send this girl back over there. I hate pimps, and I ain't far from slapping you senseless right now. Do you understand?" The bartender nodded, and Yak went back to his table. He had hardly reached his chair, when he saw the glint of a knife in the air. He whirled around and grabbed her wrist.

"Let me go," she screamed. "I kill you."

Yak walked her to the wall and held her against it. "I've got nothing against you, Astoria. I reckon you're just doing what your masters tell you to do, but I can't abide a pimp." He wrapped his free arm around her waist and kissed her warmly. She dropped the knife and seemed confused. "That's just to let you know there's no hard feelings."

* * *

In spite of all his past injuries, Yak had tried his hand at stunting, and his first taste of movie life came in San Antonio. The year 1924 brought him to Los Angeles and a stunt job in *Thundering Hoofs*. The day was wearing long, when Yak approached the director and said, "I'm not so sure about this wagon stunt, Al."

Rogell sat in a folding chair, his thinning hair swept straight back over his head, and the script in his hand. "It's just a jump from one horse to another. I've seen you do it."

"Yeah, but this time it ain't me. It's the star of the film, and he's jumping onto a team of horses."

"Oh, for heaven's sake, Fred Thompson is an Olympic athlete. He could do this in his sleep. Besides, our customers are getting wise to the fact that we substitute stuntmen. They want to believe the stars are doing these gags. He'll make the jump, pull the team to a stop, and get down. That's simple enough." He rolled the script up and pointed it at Yak. "Are you telling me you didn't teach him how to do it?"

"No. I taught him everything one man can teach another about this stunt. I'm just telling you it worries me, and you should let me do it. It's like you said. He's an athlete, and I'm afraid he's going to take the jump for granted." Yak kicked the dirt in his frustration.

"Look, Fred's got a wife and kids. Let me do the stunt, and I won't charge you a cent."

"All right, I'll do this much. You can ride on the camera truck with me. If you see something you don't like, we'll stop the shoot and fix it. How's that?"

"That's fair enough." The truck offered barely enough room for the cameraman to sit between Yak and Rogell. They started slowly down the dirt road and increased speed as the wagon neared. A beautiful, white horse thundered up beside the wagon with Fred Thompson riding hard. And, Yak began to talk to himself. "You're too wide, Fred." He turned to Rogell and said, "He's too wide." But the director didn't seem to hear. Again, Yak looked back to Silver King and Thompson and he yelled to Rogell. "Stop the scene. He's gonna fall. Stop it." Yak waved his arm and tried to stand. "Fred, pull up." His warning came too late. Thompson leapt from his horse and missed the landing. The wagon team trampled over him, and then the wagon wheels. It was Yakima Canutt's worst nightmares. He was only a stuntman, but, somehow, he felt responsible. Could he have done more?
By the time Yak and Rogell could get back to Thompson, the first-aid truck was there. "Is it bad?" Yak asked, but the medic did not answer. So, Yak knelt by Thompson and tried to comfort him as best he could.

Thompson asked only one question before he passed out. "Did we get the shot?"

Yak answered with tears on his face. "We got it, Fred. You did great."

The ambulance drove away, and Rogell called out to the crew. "Okay, that's a wrap for today. I'll see all of you in the morning."

"Is that it, Al? Don't you care about what just happened?"

"Of course, I do. I'm insulted that you'd even ask me that. Thank God, they don't think he has any internal injuries, but we've got a picture to finish, and I just lost my star. We need to figure out what we're going to do until his legs heal and figure it out fast."

Yak thought about the things Rogell said, and he knew he was right. This was business now. "Okay, I've got some ideas, and I'll put them together tonight, after I get home from the hospital. Meet me here before the crew reports in the morning, and I'll show you what I've got."

"Are you trying to be the director now?"

"You know better than that. Fred is a good man, and he's down for a while. I'm trying to save this picture for him, and for you, but I have one condition."

"Condition? I don't generally take ultimatums from stunt people, but I'm a little desperate here. So, what is it?"

"We do the stunt my way. No questions, no changes. We do it exactly the way I design it."

Rogell paused, lit a cigar, and said, "I'll see you in the morning. And, it will be your way."

* * *

Audrea Rice was no longer a child, but a painfully-thin teenager, and she was troubled by something she'd heard from her friends. She finished making her bed and decided this was the day she would ask her parents the question she didn't know how to ask. As she entered the front room, she found them seated on the sofa, each with a different section of the newspaper. "Breakfast will be ready soon, sweetheart," her mother said. "The biscuits are just about done."

"Uh, is there anything new in the paper today?" Claude answered without looking up. "Well, do you remember the guy you asked me about when you were little?"

Audrea sat on an ottoman and asked, "What guy?"

"You know, the one they called Yakima."

"Yes, I remember him. He's the rodeo champion. Everybody knows him."

"Well, it looks like he's getting into the movie business. I know how much you like westerns and Fred Thompson, but the radio said he took a bad fall, and they say this Yakima guy is going to do his stunts now. I don't know how they're going to pull that off. I mean, Fred isn't going to let somebody do his stunts."
Her teenage instincts took over, and Audrea blurted out her question. "Are you my real parents?"

They both lowered their papers, and their gazes locked on her. "Of course, we are, dear. That's your daddy, and I'm your mama. It's always been that way."

But Claude shook his head. "No, Hannah, she's not a child anymore. It's time she knew. We adopted you when you were a baby, but there's not a child in this world that is loved more than we love you."

Her emotions swelled, not knowing how much of her life had been a lie, and she fought to keep from crying. "Who were my real parents?"

"I don't know what to tell you. Your daddy is the only father you ever had. The man that put your mother in the family way took off. We don't know who he is or where he went. Your mother gave you up for adoption, and then she was killed in a car wreck. Her name was Melanie."

Claude let out a heavy sigh. "Do you want me to see if I can find your father?"

Audrea sat for a moment, then she shook her head, and said, "Let's go check on those biscuits."

* **

Fred Thompson was heavily sedated, so Yak's visit was short. He took a cab back to his trailer at the movie lot and spent the next four hours working out the details for the stunt that had nearly killed the star. He sketched rough diagrams of the neck yoke and tongue, and then the undercarriage of the wagon. Once he was satisfied with the design, he was off to bed, but rose before dawn. He met Rogell at the wagon and showed him the drawings. "I want leather straps connected here and here and here."

"I don't understand, Yak. Why do you need all that when all you have to do is jump on the team and pull them to a stop?"

"Because I'm not going to just pull them to a stop. Fred fell after he landed on the horse, right?"

"Yes."

"Then the camera can pick up as he is starting to fall. We'll start today with me on the lead team, falling, but I'm going to fall between the two teams to the ground."

"Whoa, whoa. I'm not interested in getting you run over too."

"Neither am I, and that's why I need these straps. When I first hit the ground, I'll grab the strap under the tongue. Once I stop bouncing around, I'll let go, and slide past the horses. And, that's where the strap under the kingpin comes in. I catch hold of it and pull myself up. The camera can get a shot looking down at me, but my face will be hidden under the rigging."

Rogell looked through the drawings again and said, "This sounds crazy, but it would be a great stunt. Nobody's ever done anything like this. People will go nuts for it."

"And, they'll all think Fred did it. We owe him that much." The crew started to arrive, and Rogell called over the cameraman and wagon drivers. Then his craftsmen went to work on the straps.

Within an hour, the sun was fully up, cameras were in place, and they were ready. Yak lay on one of the horses until the wagon reached full speed. At the call of action, he slipped off. But things didn't go as smoothly as he'd hoped. He squeezed between horses and felt the tremble of hoofs pounding beside his head. He began to doubt himself, but it was too late to back out now. The rough ground tore at his back, as he clung to the strap, wondering when he would stabilize enough to complete the stunt. And, finally, he just let go. The wagon passed by quicker than he planned, but he still managed to find the strap at the kingpin. With dust flying and boots dragging, he pulled himself up and found the reins. He stood on the backs of two horses and pulled the coach to a stop just short of a cliff. In spite of his cuts and bruises, he felt great. He'd designed and performed a stunt no one had done before. And, now it was in his blood, as much as bronc busting, maybe more. But he was not warmly welcomed.

At the end of the day, two other stuntmen met him at his car. "You're the guy who doubled for Fred Thompson, ain't you?'

"Yeah, Yakima Canutt, it's good to meet you. You're kind of big guys. What kind of stunts do you do?"

"Oh, same as you. You know, fights, falling off building, horses. That kind of stuff. I'm Gabe Hammond, and this is Smokey Stackhouse. We saw what you did, and we'd like to buy you a drink."

"Well, thanks, fellas. I'm trying to cut back on my drinking, but I don't guess it would hurt to have one or two with you guys."

"Yeah, a good drink never hurt anybody. Just follow my truck, and we'll show you a good place." They drove twenty minutes before they reached a row of single-story buildings, some falling down in disrepair. And, they parked in an alley, draped in darkness, but for a single light bulb. As they stepped out of the truck, Hammond held out a bottle and said, "Let's take a couple of shots before we go to the bar."

Yak let his right arm hang loose by his side, as he took the bottle with his left. As he raised it to his lips, Hammond took a swing at him, but Yak dodged it. He grabbed Hammond's shirt and punched him hard in the face. The big man fell like a redwood. Stackhouse caught him with a left to the face, but Yak sent another right that laid him beside his partner. Yak knelt by each of them and poured whiskey over their faces to bring them around. "All right, boys, do you want to tell me what this is all about?"

"You're stealing our work," Hammond answered. "You and all them other cowboys. There ain't one of you that's paid your dues to be a stuntman, but the studios give you our work anyhow."

"Look, boys, I'm just trying to make a living. Just like you."

"What did you hit me with?"

"Brass knuckles. I keep a set in the dash. This ain't the first time somebody's invited me out for a drink and then tried to beat my brains in. I ran into this same kind of deal when I first started in rodeo. Had some fellas who wanted to beat some sense into me then too, but I gave them the same medicine I gave you. I'm here to stay, boys."

Hammond worked his way to one knee and offered his hand. "You'll have no more trouble from us. Will you shake on it?"

"Sure. Bygones are bygones. We'll be pals, just so long as you remember what happened here."

* * *

Yakima continued to excel at rodeos and in 1925 he came back to Los Angeles to meet with Ben Wilson. The office was unimpressive, but Yak had come to listen, not to judge. He rolled a cigarette as Wilson lit his cigar. "Let me start by thanking you for coming, Mr. Canutt."

"You can call me Yak, if you want. Everybody does."

"And, please call me Bill. I hope we are going to be great friends. Do you know who I am, Yak?"

"They tell me you run a movie production company."

That's right, Burwillow Studios, and we're about to launch a series of westerns. The reason I wanted to talk with you today is that people say you might be the man to star in them."

"Me, star in a movie? I don't know about that."

"Don't be so quick to turn this down. People are pouring out to see pictures these days. It's not just a novelty anymore. Do you know Tom Mix?"

"Sure, everybody in the rodeo business knows Tom. I was at his house last week, trying out his ponies. Is Tom the one who called you?"

"He's one, but there were others. Did he tell how much money he's making from his pictures?"

"No, but he's got one heck of a ranch. He must be doing all right."

"And, you could do all right, too, Yak, if you apply yourself. I saw the stunts you did doubling Jack Hoxie in *Lightning Bryce*, and I was more than impressed. The other thing that draws me to you is the fact that so many people already know your name. They'd come to your movies, but they'll want to see some pretty spectacular riding and, you know, cowboy stuff."

"Well, that I can do. I just don't know about the acting part."

"We can teach you that. Besides, the focus of these films is action, lots of it. The first picture is called *Ridin' Man*, and we start shooting in two weeks. The crew is already working on the sets up in Lone Pine. We'd need for you to do your own stunts."

Yak crushed his smoke in an ashtray, stood, and walked to the end of Wilson's desk. "I can do all the stunts you want, but I want to have a say in how they're designed."

"Why would you want to do that? There's no extra money in it."

"I had the chance to go to the Indianapolis 500 a couple of years ago, and I saw a man burned to death in a wreck. It was the worst thing I've ever seen, and I don't want anything like that in my stunts, not for me and especially not for anybody else. We might break a few bones, but nobody dies."

"I'm glad to hear you say that. We don't want that either. Our pictures need lots of action, lots of excitement, but from a business point of view, fatalities are expensive. We can't take all the risk out of these stunts, and some people are going to get hurt, maybe you, but nobody gets killed."

"And, one more thing. I won't hurt the horses. That means no running W's."

"Look, westerns are new to me. What's a running W?"

"It's when they connect a cable to the horse's harness and run him a full speed. When they get to the end of the cable, the rider is thrown over the horse's head. The rider knows it's coming, and he lands in soft ground, but the horse is ruined. A lot of them get killed."

"But we need that stunt."

"I've hated that stunt from the first time I saw it. I'll show you how to do the same gag without hurting the horse. You don't have to sacrifice a good animal to get the effect you want."

Wilson paused for a moment and said, "That sounds like it could save some money. As long as it doesn't take away from the quality of the stunt, you can make your own calls. The contract is right in front of you. It covers eight movies and, if they go well, we'd offer an extension."

"I'd want to be free to rodeo in my spare time."

"Of course. That would bring more publicity for our movies."

Yak read the contract, smiled, and shook his hand. "I think we just made a deal."

* * *

For the first time, the Washington cowboy used eyeliner and had makeup applied to soften the look of his rugged face. He loved filming at Lone Pine with its harsh landscape, bordered by majestic mountains. And, he still got to work with horses. Yak sat in the passenger's seat of a new Packard with Ben Wilson at the wheel. "We should be to Kernville in about an hour," he said. "The Brown company owns a hotel there, so we can stay close to the set, but there are a few things you need to know before we get there."

"Look, Ben, I know the guys and I acted up a little at that bar the other night, but you don't need to worry. We behave when it comes time to work."

"That's good to know, but it isn't what I'm talking about. Kernville is an old town and it has a reputation for being a rough town. They used to call it Whiskey Flat, if that tells you anything. Not only that, but the production company has hired a couple of fellows I'm not so sure about. The Wofford brothers. Clay is the worse of the two, and is rumored to be a knife man."

"Oh, come on, Ben. I know we pulled a joke on you, but I'm not falling for that."

"It's true, Yak. Some of these guys carry guns, and I don't mean props."

"Then why were they hired?"

"We need men who can ride and actually convince moviegoers that they're bad guys. I mean, your record isn't exactly clean, you know. You've been in fights and in jail, haven't you?"

"That I have."

"Well, all I'm trying to do is let you know, so you can be careful."

"Okay, thanks for that, but I can take care of myself. I always have." As they reached the crest of a hill, an ambulance sped by in the opposite direction, and Yak laughed. "Hey, maybe that's one of Old Clay's victims headed to the hospital." Wilson didn't laugh, but drove the rest of the trip with hardly a word between them. The hour was late when they reached the hotel, so Yak went straight to bed.

He rose early, only to find Wilson waiting for him at the breakfast table. "How did you rest, Yak?"

"Like a baby." He filled his plate with eggs, bacon, and toast and drank half his cup of coffee in one gulp. "Oh, that's good."

"We might be a man short today." Yak wasn't sure why Wilson chose to tell him that, but he nodded. "Do you remember that ambulance last night, the one you said might have one of Wofford's victims in it?"

"Sure. Don't tell it actually did."

"Apparently, there was a card game, and Wofford got into it with one of Newt Walker's hired men. I don't know his name, but he went for a gun, and Clay sliced him up. Oh, and you'll meet Walker too. Now, there's a guy you want to keep an eye on. It's like I tried to tell you, this is a rough bunch."

* * *

Somehow the flavor went out of his breakfast, and Yak left for the set hungry. He still wasn't convinced that Wilson was doing anything more than setting him up for a practical joke, but he stopped by the hardware store and bought a box of .45 cartridges, and shoved a few into his pants pocket. The first scene called for him to ride a horse down a steep hill to the edge of a river, then stop for a camera reset and cross a stream. When everything was set, he mounted, but the horse wouldn't go into the water. "Come on, boy." He gave him a taste of his spurs, but still he balked.

"I'll get him in." It was the voice of Newt Walker, and he held a stick.

Yak waved him away. "No thanks. We don't need to beat him." Something seemed very wrong, so Yak dismounted and walked to the prop truck. When he climbed back onto the horse, he said, "Let's give it another try." But Walker was still there and slapped at the horse's rump. "Cut that out, Newt. You're drunk. Now, get out of here before I take that stick to you." Walker stood for a long, silent moment, then laughed and walked away. Yak didn't see him for the rest of the day and hoped he'd gone somewhere to sleep it off. And, the next morning he was back, as they were preparing to shoot a scene in front of a country store. Yak felt the muzzle of Walker's pistol in his ribs. He looked down and saw live ammunition in the chambers of the gun. "Be careful with that thing, Newt. It's loaded."

"A gun ain't much good if it ain't loaded." He slipped the revolver back into its holster and said, "Let's me and you go out back and have a drink."

"Sure, why not?" He put his hand on Walker's shoulder and walked around the building like they were old friends. When they reached an old outhouse, Yak said, "Hey, Newt, I've got to go. I'll be right back." He didn't wait for an answer, but stepped inside and closed the door. He unloaded the blanks from his six-shooter and replaced them with the cartridges he took from his pocket.

As he came out, he saw Waling standing with one hand resting on the hilt of his gun and the other wrapped around a bottle of whiskey. "Which hand you figure you want, cowboy?" he asked.

Yak didn't hesitate. He drew his gun, cocked it, and had the barrel in Walker's face faster than even he knew he could do. "Take a good look, Newt. Those ain't blanks in there. Now, why don't you pick a hand?" Walker loosened his gun belt and let it drop to the ground. He offered Yak the bottle and said, "I didn't mean no harm. I was just funning."

"Yeah, well, someday your funning is going to get you killed." He took a long swig from the bottle and said, "Thanks for the drink. Now, we'd better get back to work."

* * *

Yakima worked with Ben Wilson for two years, and then branched out to other studios. In 1926, Fred Jackman offered the lead role in *The Devil Horse*. They shot the movie in Montana near the Little Bighorn River. Jackman walked past the camera to the fallen log, where Yak sat with a cup of coffee, his clothes dripping wet. "That was really good, Yak. I've never had the star of a movie who was willing to jump forty feet from a cliff into a river. But you just did and, well, we need for you to do it again."

"Did the cameraman not get it?"

"Yes, he got it, but it was a side shot, from a distance. I'd like to build a stand for the camera and shoot the scene from above. That way the audience can watch it as if they were with you. It would draw them into the scene."

"Okay. I'll jump it again, but if you want any more, it's going to cost you more money."

"I think we can get it in one more take. Now, after the jump, we'll shoot the scene where you are tied to a tree, and Rex comes to your rescue."

Yak set his coffee aside. "We need to talk about this one."

"Talk about it? What do you mean?"

"I mean we need to talk about Rex. He's a fine animal, but his reputation is bad."

"Don't believe everything you hear, Yak. We've used him on a number of movies. People love Rex the Wonder Horse. He's as much a star as you are, maybe more."

"Well, your star trampled his trainer to death. And, what about that deal in *Black Cyclone*?"

"I'm sure I don't know what you're talking about."

"He went after Big Boy Williams, nearly killed him and then threw one of the actresses over a fence. He's one of those horses that seems to be calm most of the time, and then he just decides to charge somebody."

"This is an important scene, and we have a contract. Do I need to hire another actor to take your place?"

"Don't give me that. We're half way through this picture. You're not going to start over with somebody new, and I intend to honor my contract. All I saying is that I'm going to have an understanding with that horse before you tie me to a tree with him."

Jackman turned a curious look. "You want to have an understanding with a horse? And, how does one go about that?"

101

"You give me a half hour with him in the training barn. When we come out, he'll call me Mr. Canutt, and we'll shoot your scene."

"You know Rex hates a barn. He does much better in a corral, where he doesn't feel trapped."

"That's one reason I want him there." Jackman seemed unsure, but he relented. The barn offered a place where Rex wouldn't run off, but there was plenty of room for him to rear up and maul Yak to death, so he backed him into a stall. Even the stall was wide enough for Rex to kick, but this cowboy knew something about horses. The whip was not to beat Rex, but a tool to get his attention. And, the cue stick in the corner was there in case Yak didn't understand horses as well as his thought he did. He held the whip handle, let the thong droop down the side of his leg, and just waited.

It didn't take long for Rex to get anxious and try to bite him. Yak spoke to him in a stern voice. "Behave yourself." And, he slapped the handle knot across his nose. Rex pulled back as if to rear up, but Yak stepped closer and wrapped his arms around his face. Rex shook his head and then his body, but Yak held on. They wrestled around the stall until the great stallion finally shook him loose. Once more, Yak said "Behave yourself" and slapped his nose once more. When he locked his arms around that broad face again, Yak thought, *My God, this is a strong horse*. But he didn't want Rex to hear him say it. They crashed through the slats between the stalls, and now Rex had even more room to fight. Time and again Rex shook him loose, only to be rapped on the nose and fall right back into Yak's bearhug around his face. When it was over, the two walked out of the barn side by side, like old friends.

Jackman hurried over to them. "Is everything okay?"

Yak stopped and stroked the side of the horses' face. "This is a good horse. He just didn't know it. He says he's sorry for all the trouble he's caused and he won't act up again." Yak handed Jackman the reins and said, "You might want to give me a few minutes to catch my breath before I jump off that cliff again."

Chapter Five

The Devil Horse opened in LA, and Yakima sat in the back of the theatre, hoping not to be recognized. He wanted to see the movie as others did and to see their reactions for himself. When the movie ended, he exited through the lobby and thought no one noticed, but then he heard Ben Corbin's voice. "Hey, Yak."

Yak held out a hand to quiet him and said, "How are you, Ben?"

"Did you come to see how you look on the screen? Well, I can tell you this, you're just as ugly up there as you are down here, even with all that makeup."

"Well, you know how it is." He pressed his hat onto his head, and people began to gather, some holding out slips of paper for an autograph, and other reaching out to touch him. "This is what I was trying to avoid, Ben. Can you help me get out of here?"

Corbin took his elbow and began pushing admirers aside. As they made their way outside, they broke into a trot and ran down an alley. "Turn right at the corner and then duck into the first bar you see. I know the place. We'll be okay there." Corbin found a table, and the waitress brought them a bottle of tequila. "Wow, Yak, I knew you were making movies, but when did you get to be a star?"

"I can't figure it. To me, it's just another job, but people get all stirred up about it. I mean, we had people buying us drinks and all after rodeos, but this is crazy. I can't buy a can of beans without some gal saying she wants to move in with me."

"Well, you're a leading man. Stuntmen like me don't get that kind of attention."

"I'm doing stunts too, Ben. That was me Rex tossed off on his butt." They talked and reminisced until they were half way through the bottle, and a big man in bib overalls staggered to their table.

"Hey, are you that movie guy?"

Yak grinned and said, "Nope."

The man reeled, straightened up, and gave a curious turn of the head. "Yeah, you are. I saw you. Don't lie to me."

"He ain't lying," Ben answered. "This is my friend, Algernon."

Yak look past the man to the bartender, who was turning the crank on the telephone. "Uh oh, I think that guy is calling somebody we don't want to see. Come on, Ben, let's get out of here." He tried to stand, but the man pushed him back down.

"You think you're a tough guy, cowboy? Me and my buddies will whip you boys right now."

Yak looked at Corbin and then back to the man. "Look, let's be friends. What do you say?"

"All right. That suits me."

Yak stood, as the man extended his hand, but he didn't shake it. Instead, he punched him hard in the face. The man tumbled over backwards, three of his friends rushed from the bar, and the melee was on. Punching and kicking and the breaking of tables ensued for ten minutes, before a bevy of policemen broke through the door with Billy clubs in hand. A ruddy-faced sergeant grabbed Yak's collar and said, "Do I need to break your skull?"

"No, sir, I'll come peaceably."

"Good, then let's go.?" He took Yak out a side door, away from the others being arrested, to a black sedan parked by the curb. "Get in the backseat and get out of sight."

Yak wasn't sure what to make of this arrest. He wasn't in handcuffs and he wasn't riding in a paddy wagon. He lay across the bench seat and asked, "What's going on?"

"I'm not really sure myself. We were on our way home from dinner at my favorite café, after I took my wife and daughter to see your movie. My girl just turned sixteen, and she's your biggest fan. I'm not going to let her read about you being arresting in tomorrow's newspaper. A fine example you turned out to be."

"Oh, man, I'm really sorry about that. I was out with a friend, and we didn't start that trouble, but I sure hate for your daughter to hear about this. It makes me ashamed. I'm sorry." The light from scattered lampposts flickered by, as they drove down one street after another, until they finally stopped.

The policeman walked around the car and opened the back door. "Okay, Canutt, you can get out now."

Yak stepped onto the curb. "Hey, this ain't the police station. This is my hotel."

"Yeah, we know where the studios keep their property, and I may be making a big mistake here, but I'm going to give you a chance to do better without going to jail."

"I really appreciate this."

"Well, I'm not doing it for you. I don't want my daughter to see a picture of her movie hero behind bars."

"That's very decent of you, uh, say, what's your name?"

"Rice, Claude Rice."

"I don't want you to think I don't appreciate this, Claude, because I do. I come from the area around the Snake River, and we've got the biggest trout you've ever see up there. How about we go up yonder next weekend and try our hand at some fly fishing?"

Rice paused and said, "I don't normally fraternize with prisoners, but Lord, how I love to fish."

"Good, it's done then. I'll bring a tent, and all you'll need is your fishing rod."

"You ain't gonna have any movie cameras, are you?"

"No cameras, I promise. Just you and me and the fish. Yeah, I think we could be friends."

* * *

The new year opened 1927, and Yakima worried about accepting a supporting role in *Pals of the West*. He'd been the star of his movies, and Imperial was a low-budget production company. Was his popularity beginning to slide? How soon would he be just another has-been with no job and no prospects? But all that would have to wait. He settled back in his seat, a newspaper clutched in his hands, and the constant drone of train wheels rolling over the rails. The young woman is the seat facing him lowered her book and asked, "Excuse me, but are you that cowboy star?"

He smiled and answered, "I'm Yakima Canutt, if that's who you're thinking about."

"Yes, I saw you in that movie about the horse, the one that does all those tricks. What was his name?"

"Rex."

"Well, I thought you both were wonderful."

"Thank you. I appreciate that."

"You are most welcome. And, where are you headed today?"

"Seattle. I got a telegram last night that said my father had a heart attack, so I'm headed up there to check on him."

"I'm so sorry to hear that. I hope he does well."
Yak nodded and turned back to his newspaper, hoping the conversation would end. Talking about his father

was hard on any day, but especially now that his health was failing. Why had he left? No one seemed to know. His mother wouldn't talk about the divorce, and he hadn't seen his father in two years. Now, he might die before Yak could even say his goodbyes. He remembered his own divorce and how hollow it made him feel. Did anyone really love anyone else? Would he grow old and die alone?

* * *

By the time Yak reached the house, time was clearly running short. He stepped from bright sunshine into a dim living room lit by a single lamp. He looked at the relatives seated around the walls, and said, "Why ain't my daddy in the hospital?" No one answered, and he turned to his father's brother. "Uncle Joe, tell me why he's at this house instead of the hospital."

Joe's wrinkled face showed few signs of emotion. He spat into a can and said, "There ain't nothing a doctor can do for him, son. They told us that before we brought him home. We figured he'd rather die here."

Yak ran his gaze across the papered walls, then took a kitchen chair and carried it into his father's bedroom. He sat down with a groan. "Daddy, can you hear me? It's Enos."

John's voice was stronger than he expected. "It's good to see you, boy."

"You know, there's a lot of people out there, and they're all waiting for you to get better. So am I."

"I won't be getting better. That's the God's truth." He paused to take a labored breath and said, "I'm dying and I know it, but I'm sure glad to see you before I go. I want to, well, I want to tell you I'm sorry for walking out on you and your brothers and sisters. I didn't want to go."

"Then why did you? I don't understand. What happened with you and Mama?"

"Don't blame her. Whatever you do, don't blame you mother."

"Was it that woman, that Pearl?"

"And, don't blame Pearl either. She's a good person."

"Hold on. You're a good person, Mama is good, Pearl is good. If everybody is so good, how come our family fell apart?" Then Yak realized there were no good answers and he was wasting his last minutes with his father over things that would not change. "You know, I just finished another picture, and we're starting a new one in a couple of months. They say talking movies are coming soon, and that'll change everything. But don't let that worry you. I can still make money doing stunts."

The old man struggled for each breath. His gaze ran to the window, and he said, "Enos, do you believe in heaven?"

Yak knew the end was at hand and he needed to choose his words carefully. "Yes, Daddy. I believe in heaven, and I believe you'll go there. Don't be afraid."

And, John Canutt's life ended with two words. "Not afraid."

* * *

The mourners at Evergreen Cemetery included two of John's sons, his brother Joe, Pearl, and a few others Yak didn't know. The simple headstone bore his name and a space for his second wife to be buried beside him. The minister finished his remarks, and two workmen started filling the grave, as the onlookers began to leave. Yak didn't speak to Pearl. Why should he? She was the woman who broke up his home, or at least he believed she was. He lit a cigarette and turned to his brother. "He should've been buried on the ranch, Alex. Next to Grandpa and Granny."

"I know, but Pearl wouldn't have it, and she is his legal wife, you know. Besides, Mama didn't want him there either."

"Did she tell you that?"

"In just those words. She said a man who runs out on his family doesn't deserve to be buried with them."

"Well, I'm not so sure he ran out on us. She remarried two years before he did."

Alex grabbed the front of Yak's jacket and growled, "What are you trying to say?"

"I'm not saying anything, but you need to take your hands off me, brother. We're not kids anymore, and I'll slap you right off your feet." Alex let go and leaned against his cane. "That's better. If you think I meant Mama was cheating on him, I don't. But she married

111

that Welty guy pretty darn quick. She didn't give Daddy a chance to fix things. All I'm saying is that she could've given him a better chance, especially after twenty-five years." He scooped up a handful of dirt and tossed it onto his father's casket. "What about the others? I thought at least Sally would come."

"She wanted to, but we only had enough money for one train ticket. It's a long way from the ranch to Everett, and I'm the oldest."

"Look, if you guys need money, I'm doing okay right now. Is Henry not working?"

"Seems like he came down with a mysterious ailment just about the time he married Mama. Sore back, stomach problems, you know. Sally married that Finley boy, so she left. But I'm still working down at the mercantile, and we bring in a couple of Chinese at harvest time."

"What about John and Rita."

Alex fastened the button on his jacket and said, "What are you doing, Enos? You took off and never looked back. And, now that Daddy's gone, you start asking about the family, like you really give a rat's behind."

"I do care about them, Alex, and I care about you. I sent money home to Mama until I had to start paying support to Kitty, and then there wasn't anything left to send. Besides, I've been home a couple of times."

"Yeah, a couple of times. Maybe you wouldn't hate Henry so much, if you got to know him."

"I don't hate Henry. I just don't think he had any business marrying my mother. That's all." He crushed his smoke on the bottom of his boot and thought about the things he'd said. "I'm sorry, Alex. I guess I need to do better. I reckon I ought to do that much for Mama."

"She reads about you in the newspapers, you know. The rodeos, the movies."

"Yeah?"

"Yes, and the times you've been arrested. Your drunkenness, the fights you get into."

"That's all behind me now. I grew up a lot in the Navy, and watching all those people die from influenza showed me how fragile life can be. I'm not the man I used to be."

"Then show it, Enos. Show it to your mama."

* * *

For the next few years, Yakima lived the life of a nomad, never really at home anywhere, and as lonely as his thirty-five years could teach him to be. Talkies pushed silent movies into obscurity, and that was a problem. His bout with influenza damaged his throat. At times he would mouth a word, but nothing came out, and talkies needed dialogue. But he was not to be beaten. He approached Mascot Productions and convinced them that more action would bring people out to see their pictures, and he was the man to make that happen. So, they took a chance on him. He made enough money to survive, but not much more, nothing

113

like he had made in his silent movies. Still, he was working in a time when most men were idle during the Great Depression, and the movie industry struggled. Between working on serials at Mascot he rodeoed, and he was always on the move. One evening his close friend and fishing buddy Claude Rice invited him home for dinner.

His plate sat on the modest table, smeared with the remains of chicken, mashed potatoes, and green peas. "That's the best meal I've had since I left Mama." Rice folded his napkin and said, "Well, you can thank Audrea there for that. Her mother's at a church meeting tonight, and my little girl cooked the whole thing."

"Oh, Daddy, I'm not a little girl. I'm twenty-three for goodness sake."

She was the most beautiful girl he'd ever seen, and Yak wasn't sure what he should say. "Twenty-three? That's a good age. I mean, you know, for a girl, I guess. I don't see a ring on your finger, so I'm thinking you're not married. Not that you should be. Twenty-three is still young. Are you engaged or anything?"

She demurred and said, "No. Things just never seemed right. I suppose I shall be an old maid."

"Not you. A man would be crazy not to want you for a wife."

Audrea smiled, and her father said, "Sweetheart, why don't you go out to the kitchen and get us some coffee?" He waited for her to leave. "You know, she's been a fan of yours since she was a child, Yak."

"I remember you telling me that on the night you decided not to arrest me."

"Yeah, boy. She saw every one of your movies as a child. Even kept a scrapbook."

"You don't say. Well, ain't that something, but I reckon she got over that. She's not a child anymore." Yak stood and started clearing the table.

"Don't bother with that. Audrea will do it."

"I don't guess it'll hurt me to help out. After all, she cooked the whole dinner. I'll just carry these out to the kitchen for her." Rice shrugged, and Yak left, balancing dishes between his arms. He found Audrea by the sink with her back turned. His gaze ran over her slim figure and the long, strawberry hair spilling down her back. She was a grown woman with an innocence about her, so different from Kitty, so different from the other women he'd known. His heart warmed, and he loved her at once. "Uh, if you'll excuse me, I'll put these in the sink."

"Oh, you startled me."

"I sure didn't mean to do that." She stepped to one side, but she was still close enough for him to smell the scent of her perfume, as he set the dishes down. "Can I ask you something, Audrea?"

"Sure. Ask away."

"I've got to go east for rodeos in New Jersey and a couple other places. So, it's gonna be a while before I get back to LA. Would you mind if I wrote you while I'm gone?"

Her face seemed to come to life with a smile as genuine as a mother's love. "I wouldn't mind at all. Is there someone who handles your mail when you're on the road, so I could write you back?"

"That would be swell. I'll give you a list of the cities and dates. You can reach me through General Delivery. I'll check with them every day."

"Do you always check on your mail every day?"

"No, ma'am, I don't. I almost never check the mail, but I will now."

"I heard what my father said in there, you know, about the scrapbook and I want you to understand something. I'm not a twelve-year-old anymore and I'm looking for a lot more in a relationship than being a fan. I'm a grown woman."

"Yes, you are. I can surely see that."

* * *

With his east-coast contract completed, Yakima packed his valise with his clothes and Audrea's letters, and he came back to Los Angeles. All his aspirations, his championships, his movies took second place to the policeman's daughter. She was all he wanted, but times were tough. The weeks passed, and their romance grew. In the early evening of a September day, they sat on a rocky precipice overlooking the open waters of the Pacific Ocean. Audrea took his hand and asked, "How did you get that scar on your lip?"

"That came from a bull at Pendleton ten years ago. I landed on him wrong, and his horn cut my mouth up really bad."

"And, after that you decided to go back to bulldogging?"

"The next day. The rodeo doctor stitched me up and he put gun cotton in the bandage. I tried to light a cigarette and nearly blew my face off."

"Nooo."

"It's the God's honest truth. I wouldn't lie to you. Now, Tom Mix would. That man is the biggest liar I ever met, not in a harmful way. He just likes to spin yarns, and he's really good at it." He pointed to a scar over his left eyebrow. "I got this one in a fight at Fort Dodge, Iowa. Some of us liked to get to the rodeos early, so we had time to kill, and we'd play cards or gamble. The guys had a dice game going in a barn, and I went mainly to watch. There were three men I'd never seen, but I was sure they were cheating. Their dice were odd, kind of green and red. I left the game and found a shop that sold the same kind of dice. Then I took them to a dentist and had him drill the spots deeper, fill them with platinum, and tint them white."

He paused and said, "I don't want you to misunderstand. I like an honest game, but sometimes cheats need a taste of their own medicine. Anyway, I went back, took their money, and divided it among the other cowboys. Of course, the cheats were waiting for me when I left."

"So, you fought with the three crooks?"

"I guess they thought they'd whip me good, if they got me alone, but Ben Corbett was close by. I got this scar, but I can promise you they left with a whole lot more." Then it occurred to him this may not be the best way to win a girl's heart. The silence was awkward, and he wondered what he should say next, but he took a chance. "There's something I've been wanting to ask you, but I'm not sure I should."

She gave him a knowing look and said, "Ask whatever you want, and I'll answer you as best I can."

"Well, first I should be honest with you. I don't have a lot other than debts, but I do have steady work lately, and I'd never let you do without. I want you to know that. In fact, I've got an appointment at Lone Star Productions tomorrow. And, Kitty remarried, so I don't have to pay alimony anymore."

"Yak, are you giving me a financial report or are you asking me to marry you?"

"Uh, yeah, that's it. I mean the marry-me part."

"I want to say yes, with all my heart, but I need to know something. There are times when I don't understand you. It seems like, if you're not getting beat up by some steer, then you've been in a fight. What's going on with you?"

"That's hard to say. It's like I'm trying to find something, and I just don't know what it is. It's frustrating. So, I ride hard and live hard, hoping somehow I might run into it." He ran a finger down the long scar on his arm, a reminder of a steer's horn, and reflected for a moment. "I have this recurring nightmare. Someone is chasing me and, when I turn around, it's me."

"I understand."

"Really, Audrea? Do you really?"

"It's in your blood. You told me about your grandfather crossing the plains in a wagon and never turning down a fight. Running the ranch was never enough for your father. He had to be in the legislature, until he actually was in the legislature. Then he had to get involved in the governor's race. When it was over, he was about to go stir crazy before you got into rodeo, and that gave him something else to get excited about. I guess it's that way with you Canutt men." She stroked the side of his face. "And, I guess I'll have to get used to it, because it will probably be that way with our children."

* * *

He couldn't have been more pleased than he was, when Yakima arrived on set the next morning. His engagement to Audrea lifted his spirits in a way he had not known for a very long time, if at all. But the weight of that engagement was not lost to him. He needed steady work to support a wife and maybe a family, and it came at a time when millions of men stood in breadlines. Robert Bradbury met him on the movie set, and they walked toward his trailer together. "I'll be directing this film, Yak. It's called *Rider of Destiny*, and

119

it's the first of maybe a dozen quickies we want to make with this new, young actor. Well, that assumes he's going to work out, but we think he will. What we need from you is to give us some good stunts and teach this guy to ride a horse."

"The stunts I can do, but he's going to have to want to learn to ride. What's his name?"

Bradbury pushed the trailer door open and said, "That's him in the chair. I'll introduce you."

A tall, young man stood and smiled broadly. "Well, Yakima Canutt, you old dog."

"My gosh, you didn't tell me it was John Wayne."

Bradbury laughed lightly. "He asked me not to tell you, so it would be a surprise. The truth is John specifically asked for you to be in this movie."

"Yak and I worked together in a series called *Shadow of the Eagle*. He doubled me in a stunt where he jumped from a motorcycle to a car. When I saw that, I knew I wanted to work with this guy again."

"Well, that's very kind of you, John. Mr. Bradbury tells me you want to learn how to ride, but I thought you already knew how."

"I know how to get into the saddle and not fall off, but this movie calls for me to ride at full speed right in front of the camera, and all I do is bounce around."

"We can fix that." He turned to Bradbury. "I read the script last night. It's a good story, but some of the stunts look a little weak. If it won't offend the writers, I'd like to spice them up."

"Don't worry about the writers. They work for me. You're about the same size as John, so you'll double him in most of the stunts. I'll leave it up to you guys to work out the details. Oh, yes, I nearly forgot. You'll have a few lines too, Yak."

"I'll give it a try, but I watched the movie John was talking about, and my voice sounds like a hillbilly in a well."

Wayne wrapped his arm around Yak's shoulders and said, "I want you to teach me how you talk and how you walk."

"Are you sure about that?"

"You're a real cowboy. I just play one. I want that swagger, that deliberate way you say things. If I can translate that onto the movie screen, then I'll have something the others don't have. Something movie-goers will remember."

"I expect Mr. Bradbury has things to do. Why don't we go outside and get started?" Yak and Wayne left the trailer and stopped at the bottom of the steps. "Say, John, I noticed that this movie opens with you riding across the prairie singing."

"Yeah. My character is called Singin Sandy."

"I don't mean to hurt your feelings, but there ain't no stunt double in the world who could make you sound like a singer."

"I know. I tried to tell Bradbury that, but he's determined to have a singing cowboy. Maybe they'll cut that scene once he hears me."

121

"For your sake, I hope so."

* * *

Yak stayed busy for the next year, doubling for stars like Douglas Fairbanks and Gene Autry, but the bulk of his time was spent at Monogram with John Wayne. Most of his work had been devoted to designing and performing stunts, with occasional, small roles as a henchman. Normally, he wore an old pair of blue jeans with a faded shirt, but today he came to Lone Pine dressed in one of his bright rodeo outfits. He found the coffee pot, poured a cup, and sat beside Wayne on a bench. "Well, I'm guessing I have you to thank for this part, John," he said.

"You have yourself to thank. I just spoke to the director. You showed me what you can do in the last three movies we did. It was time for you to have a bigger part, and that quirky voice of yours is perfect for the villain."

"Have they got a title for this one yet?"

"The last I heard it's going to be called *Sagebrush Trail*, but I also heard *An Innocent Man*. What did you think of the plot?"

"I like it a lot, and I see where we can do a lot with the fight scenes and stunts."

"We?"

"Yeah, I've seen your work in the last three movies too. You understand camera angles. If we set them right, we can throw punches that look real. And, well, I don't want this to sound the wrong way, but you've grown up. You're not the twenty-five-year-old I met in *Shadow of an Eagle*."

Wayne laughed and said, "Well, I'm still a lot younger than you."

"I know that well enough. I'm pushing forty now, and I've got this bald spot in the back of my head to prove it."

"That's not so old. You look in great shape."

"I am, the best shape of my life, and I have to be. The studio wants better gags, riskier gags, and I've got to be smart about them. I can't keep getting busted up or my movie career will end pretty quick. Most of this movie is okay. I've got to fall over a horse's head into a lake, make a couple of scissors mounts, and jump onto a moving stage coach."

"You've done that before."

"Yeah. At the end of this story, they want a crash scene for the stage, a big, spectacular wreck, down a mountainside. It's going to be terrific, but I'd rather not get killed doing it."

"Did they say how the trick is supposed to work? I mean, they have engineers."

"Engineers are fine. They can build whatever I want, but not one of them has ever done a stunt. They don't really understand the human part of it. The directors always tell me, 'You figure it out. That's why we pay you.' And, they're right, so I've been working on it."

"Sounds like you might be a little worried about that wife of yours."

"It's different as a married man. I've got responsibilities. And, we've got the boy now, Tap."

"I thought you named him Eddie."

"We did, Edward Clay, but we call him Tap. It's short for Tapadero, the leather stirrup cover on a Mexican saddle. My brother Alex came up with that." The memory of Alex stung for a moment, but he pushed it aside. "I've never been scared to do a stunt, but this industry has got to get better at protecting its people." He drank the rest of his coffee, set the cup down, and said, "Let's talk about something else. Tell me something. How did you get the name John Wayne? I mean, they call me by my real name, Canutt, but they changed yours."

"They tried to use my real name in my first movie. They called me Duke Morrison. It was a bit part, so it didn't much matter. Then we shot *The Big Trail*. It was my first lead role, and they decided to change my name. At first, they wanted to call me Anthony Wayne, but the producer thought it sounded too Italian, so he picked John."

"Yeah, I can see why they'd do that. It wasn't too long after the Great War, and we lost a lot of men fighting with Italy."

"You were in the war, weren't you, Yak?"

"I don't talk about that. Well, I see Malvern is stirring around. I guess we'd better get to work." Yak spent the next two weeks playing "the Boss" and doubling for good guys and bad guys alike. He did falls and jumps and fights, and finally the day came to shoot the final scenes on the downgrade of a mountainside road, and Paul Malvern sought him out. "Okay, Yak, this is it. The preceding scene has the hero and his friend trying to escape from the outlaw gang in this stagecoach. You'll be driving the stage down to that curve, and then it crashes down the hill. We don't have another stagecoach, so we've got to do this in one take. Please tell me you've figured out how to do that."

"Of course, I have."

"Good. What's the plan?"

"You told me to figure it out, and I did. There's a cable tied to a device between the front wheels. It's just long enough to reach the curve, and then it'll yank the wheels together and throw the wagon. So, just take your seat and watch. If I get killed, try not to show that part to my wife." Malvern stormed off, shaking his head, and rode away in a camera truck. Yak waited to be sure all the cameras were in place, then he boarded the stage and started down the mountain. He needed enough speed to make the coach summersault and tumble down the hill, but not enough to lose control. He snapped the reins, pushing the horses faster and faster. Somehow, he worried more about them than he did himself. As they neared the bend in the road, he leapt from the seat onto a board he'd attached to the wagon tongue, his heart racing with excitement. He reached for the lever to release the team, as the cable snapped tight and jerked the wheels, but his foot slipped. In an instant, the stage would be flipping over and over, but Yak managed to reach the lever, and he steered the horses toward one of the cameras.

Malvern ran to him, as he stepped down and said, "You scared me nearly to death."

"I meant to. I hope it scares our audience to death too."

"Yes, I hope they wet their pants. And, next time we'll do something even bigger."

* * *

"Okay, let me set the scene for all of you." It was the third time Paul Malvern had covered the same scene, but Yak knew he had to be patient. "Now, the bad guy is down there at the bottom of the mountain. John's character rides up to the cliff, ties a rope to his saddle horn, and slides down to that ledge."

"Yes, and then he jumps off the ledge into the water."

"Let me finish, Yak. Where was I? Okay, yes, he jumps off the ledge into the water. All right then, let's get started. Oh, wait, is John in place?"

Yak looked over the edge and saw Wayne standing next to a bolder, out of sight of the camera. "He's there."

"Well, then, uh, action."

The rope drew taut as Yak eased his way over the cliff, his hat pulled low to hide his face. The descent to the ledge was easy enough and, once there, he gathered himself and leaped off, but then everything went wrong. He knew he'd jumped too short and would never clear the flat rock below. He spread his arms and legs, hoping the shallow water over the rock might break his fall. It did not. The pain exploded in his right hip, and his leg went numb. His body began slipping into the deeper water, when two long arms caught him. "Is it bad?" Wayne asked.

"Bad enough. Can you help me get to the bank?"

"Sure. You just hang on." Yak was a big man, but Wayne pulled him up and dragged him to safety.

He laid him on the ground, and Yak asked, "Did they get the shot?"

"I think so."

"Well, then get out there and catch the bad guy, while we've still got a crew." They finished the shot, while Yak rode to the hospital in the back of a truck. John Wayne drove him home and helped Audrea get him into bed. Even laudanum did little to help him sleep, and the phone call at one o'clock made things even worse. Yak pulled himself into a chair and said, "Audrea, I need you to help me get dressed."

"Get dressed? Do you need to go back to the hospital?"

"No, that was Rocky Peoples. A few weeks ago, I told him I'd help with a picture they've been shooting at night, and they're ready to shoot the scene."

"You cannot be serious. Tell them to get someone else."

"I tried, but there's no time. It's a low-budget film, the crew is ready, and I need to go."

"No. You're hurt, and I won't allow this."

"I'm hurt, and you're pregnant. If I don't show up, they won't give me any jobs in the future. I don't have a choice. I'll be okay. Really. It's just one little jump."

She helped him up and into his clothes. He stretched, grinned, and nodded his head. "So, just how high is this little jump?" she asked.

"Thirty feet."

Chapter Six

John Wayne and Yakima Canutt made eight movies together in 1934, and they became fast friends in a business where true friendship was rare. They appeared in six movies the next year and a handful in 1936. Yak found work in other studios, and he thought his work with John Wayne was drawing to a close, until he was called to meet with John Ford on the set of *Stagecoach*. He found Ford with a crew of workers, trying to pull a stagecoach from a river. "Come on, men," Ford shouted. "Get that thing out of there. I've got a movie to make." He threw his cigar down and looked up from his chair. "Well, don't just stand there, whoever you are. Get out there and help."

"I'd be glad to help, Mr. Ford, and my name is Yakima Canutt."

"Canutt, yes, you're that stuntman Wayne told me about. Sit down. Right now, I've got other problems."

Yak took his seat next to Ford and asked, "Are you trying to float the stage across the river with those logs?"

"Trying and failing."

"Do you have a good machine shop close by?"

"Yes, but why do you ask?"

"You could have them mount the logs on an engine lathe and hollow them out. Then plug them back up, seal everything, and fill them with compressed air."

Ford thought for a moment and then called to one of his assistants. "Call that machinist and tell him to get out here. Pronto." He turned back to Canutt. "You're a thinking man, aren't you?"

"I try to be."

"Good, because I'm in the process of making one of the greatest movies in history, certainly the best western. This is not just some shoot-'em-up. We've got a strong story line and a cast that will knock your shoes off. Now, what we need from you are a few stunts that will add to the story. Understand me, the stunts are not to be the main focus of this movie. The plot is. The stunts are complimentary, but they need to be good."

"I understand. You won't have any problems with me. I know you work fast, and so do I."

"You'd better. This movie cannot get behind schedule. We'll be moving to a site near Victorville, California next week. Do you know it?"

"I think so. Is that where that dry lake bed is?"

"That's exactly where we'll be. The coach will be attacked by a huge band of Apache, and we need all that space to capture the epic proportions of the scene. I'll have cameras everywhere. I need some of the usual, you know, men shot off horses and the like. And, I want a couple of special stunts. One to highlight the danger, to make people believe these characters

130

are about to be massacred. Then I want something that presents Ringo, uh that's John's character, something that makes Ringo look like a real hero."

"Yes, sir, I can do that."

"See to it that you do. I'm not the kind of director that likes to be bothered with the details. I have my job to do, and you have yours. Just be sure you do it well."

Yak spent the next three days designing his stunts, and then contacted Ford's crew. They widened the space between the horses and installed boards across the tongue. He remembered the stunt he'd used in *Thundering Hoofs*, but it had to be bigger, more spectacular. He took one of his own saddles to a leather shop and had them rivet an L-shaped metal piece into its side for a step. By weeks end, he was ready.

The day arrived, and dozens of extras, dressed in Indian fare and on horseback, spread across the lake bed. It was by far the largest cast Yak had ever seen. "Boy, I need to get this right, John."

"You'll be fine," Wayne answered. "I believe in you, and so does Pappy."

"Really? Did he tell you that?"

"Well, he named one of the characters after you. It's the wife of the guy at the weigh station. She's an Apache girl named Yakima, but you pronounce it like a girl's name, Yakeema. He told me he might put you in one of the opening scenes too. Just a few lines, but he doesn't do that for people he doesn't like."

131

"Well, I guess I'd better get on the stage."

"Yeah. You're doubling me in this, right?"

"That I am, Jonathan. That I am. The driver has been shot, and the reins are hanging loose."

"Then I'll ride on the camera truck with Pappy and watch. Make me look good, Yak."

"I'll try, And, hey, when we do the other gag later today, don't let them take the camera off me until I roll over at the end. I don't want people to think we used a dummy for that stunt."

Yakima pulled the stage into position, put the horses in motion, and the cameras rolled. Once they reached full speed, he stood and braced himself against the man who was doubling the injured driver. He took a breath and leaped from the stage onto the wheel team. It was a long jump, but he landed right where he wanted to. He stepped onto the cross board and sprang forward to the middle team, but his foot landed off center, and he nearly fell. He grabbed the harness and made the jump to the swing team without thinking. Once he straddled the lead horse, the stunt was over, and it was time for John Wayne to step in.

Yak rode one of the spare horses back to the studio camp, found a cup of water, and waited for the call to do his next gag. He couldn't allow himself to think of nearly falling in the first stunt. The next one would be even more dangerous, and there was no room for doubt. Once he had collected himself, he donned Indian clothes and a wig. Then he mounted a pinto horse and joined the horde of extras. It felt like cameras were everywhere. This would be the most exciting scene in the movie, and Yak could not afford to fail. On the director's call, he kicked his horse and sped after the stagecoach, spear in hand. He felt the spirit of the scene, Apache warriors pouring around the small band of travelers. The Ringo Kid atop the stage, firing his rifle in every direction with no thought to his own safety. And, now it was Yak's time.

He pulled his horse between the stage and Ford's camera truck. He charged forward to the lead team, pulled his foot up to the saddle step, and made the longest jump of his career. His foot landed between the swing horses, as he caught their necks and jumped to the tongue. "Thank God," he whispered. Ringo turned and took a shot, and Yak fell between the horses. He hung on, his body dragging between pounding hoofs. Another shot from Ringo, and Yak let go. The horses ran past his head and then the metal-clad wheels. At last, he stopped sliding and rolled over, scraped and bruised, and thrilled with the outcome. But what would Pappy Ford think?

Once the scene was over, Yak and Wayne hurried to Ford's truck, and heard him talking to his cameramen. "Camera One, did you get the shot?"

"I'm not sure, Mr. Ford."

"Not sure? What do you think we're doing here, playing games?" He questioned each camera crew, and no one could assure him they had the entire stunt.

Yak pulled off his wig and said, "It would only take a few minutes to set up for me to do it again."

Ford looked at him with the stern eyes of a worried father. "You'll never do that stunt for me again. I'm not in the business of killing people."

"But it's perfectly safe."

"Son, I can't let you take that chance again. Let's see what the cameras got. If they missed it, we may have to cut your part." It seemed like a very long time before the film was developed and Ford had the chance to view it. When he did, he left the projection room with a smile. "We got it all, boys. It's the greatest stunt of all time."

* * *

Yak was proud of his work on *Stagecoach*, but that movie was over, and it was time to find another job. Within a week, he started to work for Sol Seigel on *Man of Conquest*. "Yakima, I want you to meet our second unit director, Breezy Eason."

"I've met Breezy before." He offered his hand, and Eason refused. "Well, I look forward to working with you. What's the first gag?"

Eason chewed on an unlit cigar and said, "You're going to drive that wagon full of explosives through the battle scene. Then it's going to blow up and throw you off."

"Is that all?"

"What do you mean, 'Is that all?' It's a stunt and you're a stuntman. Just drive the wagon." Now, leave me alone. I've got stuff to do."

Breezy walked away, and Yak turned to Seigel. "Has he been drinking again?"

"Most probably. He's really good on action scenes, but his alcohol use is a problem. That's one reason I sent for you. I need for you to hold him up."

"Well, we start by fixing this stunt. First, I can tell you by looking we've got too much dynamite in the back of this wagon. Way too much. So, let's take half of it out. Then I want some two-by-twelve boards behind the seat, so I don't get impaled by a sharp piece of wood."

Seigel motioned for a crewman. "Pay attention and do what he tells you."

Yak nodded to show his appreciation. "Okay, the shade top on the wagon will hide the two-by-twelves from the camera. I need a cable connected to the front half of the wagon. We'll rig the explosives to fire once I hit the end of the cable. We'll have a tremendous explosion, then the wagon will flip and spin on its end."

Seigel shook his head. "I don't believe you can do that."

"Fifty dollars says I can."

"You're on."

The crew spent two hours rigging the wagon, and Breezy Eason was nowhere to be found. But he was there when Yak climbed aboard. Seigel spoke through a megaphone. "Okay, everybody, let's get this right. We want people to believe they're really with Sam Houston at the Battle of San Jacinto."

Cannon fire and rattling sabers echoed off the trees surrounding the battlefield. Actors and extras clashed for five minutes, and then it was time for Yak. He drove the team toward one of the cameras. And, at the end of the cable, Yak freed the horses, and the rear of the wagon blew to pieces. He made his jump, as the wagon flipped and spun.   He lay on the ground until the rest of the scene was completed, and Seigel yelled, "Cut."

The stunt had gone better than even he expected. He reached Seigel in time to hear Eason say, "What did I tell you? When I blow up a wagon, it gets done right."

* * *

Audrea dabbed iodine onto the scrapes on Yakima's back and sides. He felt every sting, but said nothing. He was getting older, maybe too old for these kinds of stunts, and he knew. Still, he didn't want her to worry about him, so he tried to divert her attention to something else. "Are the boys in bed yet?"

"Yes, and I had a time with Tap. He always wants to see his daddy before he goes to bed."

"What about Joe?"

"He's too young to really understand how late it is, but he misses you too. I can see it in his face. He has that look."

"What do you mean?"

"I see it in him just like I see it in you. He's not much more than a baby, but he has the same passion. I can tell him no a hundred times, but he's going to do what he does."

"Yeah, he's a pistol. Oh, I got a call about another job today."

"It's not in Utah again, is it?"

"Culver City. Have you read that book, the one about the Civil War?"

"Do you mean *Gone with the Wind*?"

"That's the one. Selznick International is taking it to film. I think Clark Gable recommended me. You know, we did that movie together in '36, *San Francisco*. You remember that."

"I remember nursing you through six broken ribs. Is he going to play Rhett? Everybody says he's the only one who could." She treated another cut and sighed. "I read that book three times. You know, it breaks my heart when he walks off in the end. Poor Scarlet." She set the iodine aside and said, "You don't have to do anything dangerous, do you?"

"I guess that'll be up to me this time. They're going to let me do some directing on the action scenes."

"Oh, Yak, that's great. This could be the break you've been looking for. You always wanted to direct."

"It's been a long time coming, and this may be the only chance I get, so I need to make the most of it."

* * *

David Selznick was as unique a man as his reputation said. His round glasses and half-crook pipe made him look more like a college professor than a movie producer, but he demanded excellence from every person on the set, and he put Yak to work with Clark Gable on his first day. Gable lit a cigarette, as he leaned against a post. "Well, Yak, you're doubling me in this scene, and the deal is for Rhett to drive this horse and wagon through Atlanta with three women and a baby in it. Oh, and by the way, Atlanta is burning, courtesy of General Sherman. Now, the director will be here in a few minutes, and he's going to tell you the same thing I just told you. But I'm the star of this movie, and I need for people to believe my character is in the middle of an inferno. I mean hell on earth."

"Don't worry about that. By the time we're finished, people will wonder how you survived it. The director called me last night, and I was here at dawn, looking for props."

"Dawn? That's about the time I went to bed. So, what did you find?"

"They're putting up some store fronts behind the rail cars, but that won't be enough. So, we're going to put King Kong's wall back there and burn it."

"No kidding?"

"Oh, yeah, it's huge. Once we get it going, it might be tough to put out, but that's the fire crew's problem."

"Why don't you shoot it in front of a screen. It's a lot safer that way. That horse may not understand we're just acting."

"I've worked with horses all my life. I'll take care of him, and people are getting wise to the scenes shot in front of a screen. The people I know and respect tell me this is going to be a great movie. I don't want to take away from that with a cheap stunt."

"Okay, it's your show. I'm just glad I'm not the one who'll be holding that nag's head when Atlanta goes up in flames."

* * *

Evening came, and all Yak's props were set in place, with three firetrucks standing by. The principle actors completed their shots, and Yak stepped in, with a stuntwoman seated next to him on the wagon seat. He drove through showers of burning debris, and then Gable's dire prediction came true. The horse panicked, stopped, and reared up. There would be no chance for a retake. Yak jumped down and wrapped a black cloth over the horse's eyes. "He grabbed the reins and grunted. "Come on, boy, before we both burn." Yak wasn't sure if the horse understood, but it began to move. "That's it, keep coming, keep coming." Instead of running from the fire, they ran toward it, and then past the great wall, aflame against a dark sky. His lungs burned, and he looked up to the stuntwoman on the seat. She nodded she was okay, and they ran the full length of the fire.

When they reached safety, Yak made sure the stuntwoman and horse were safe, and then found a place to catch his breath. After a few minutes, Gable found him. "That was outstanding."

The director came out in Yak. "Did they get it all?"

"I sure hope so. I don't think you could do that again."

"No, we couldn't. We don't have another wall to burn."

* * *

"Daddy! Tap called me a poop head."

Joe was complaining to his father, but his mother answered. "Don't you dare use that kind of language in this house. Boy, I will wash your mouth with soap."

Yakima sat at his desk, loading Virginia burley into his pipe. "Joe, go get your brother, and both of you meet me in your bedroom."

"He started it."

"Yes, and you tattled on him. Brothers don't tell on each other. When I finish smoking this pipe, I'll be back there, and I'd better find you boys waiting for me."

Tap strode into the room clad in cowboy boots and hat. "I only called him that name because that's what he is."

"I am not."

"Are too."

"Cut it out, boys. Your mother's not feeling well today, and this fussing is not going to make her feel any better."

Rather than go to the bedroom and wait for their spanking, the two Canutt boys sat by their father's feet. They looked at each other, and Tap said, "We went to the movies yesterday."

"What did you see?"

"*Lucky Texan.*"

"Are they still showing that? My goodness, boys, that movie must be five or six years old."

Joe hugged his father's leg. "We saw you in it."

"You know, there's a funny part in that movie. I doubled the bad guy, when he jumped on a horse and ran away. Then I put on John Wayne's clothes and went after the bad guy." And, he saw the irony of that scene and the nightmare that haunted him so many times. "Yeah, they paid me to literally chase myself."

Joe squeezed tighter and said, "You're my favorite cowboy, Daddy."

But Tap had a different answer. "Uncle John's my favorite, but not Mama's. She likes Tim Holt, 'cause he's so handsome and has those dimples." He giggled. "Ain't that right, Mama?"

Yak smiled, but Audrea didn't answer. He set his pipe on the side table and said, "All right, you guys go get ready for bed. Daddy's got to go to work tonight."

Audrea wadded a dishcloth in her fists. "Work? I just told you I'm pregnant again, and you're going off to work?"

"Well, yeah. It's an outdoor shot, and we need it to be dark." The air in the room felt heavy. He waited till

141

she hurried the children down the hallway to their bedrooms and came back with a look on her face only an angry wife could have. "You know I've got to take the jobs when I can get them, especially with a new baby coming."

"Don't you dare use this baby as an excuse to go off and leave me alone."

"What do you expect me to do, Audrea? The whole company will be there tonight, and they expect me to show up to double Gable. There's not enough time to find somebody else."

"What about Ben Corbin?"

"He's not tall enough, and I don't even know where he is tonight." He stood and took her hands in his. "Look, John Waters is directing this movie. You know John. He's a good guy, and I already told him how to set up the stunt. It won't take thirty minutes to shoot it. I'll be home before you know it."

For a moment, he thought he'd said the right things to calm her. Then she pulled away, turned her back, and said, "You do whatever you're going to do. I'll take care of myself."

"All right, if that's how you want it, that's how it'll be." He slammed the door as he left, climbed into his Pierce Arrow, and drove across town to the studio. A full moon hung over the set. *That's appropriate*, he thought. *The evil spirits are out tonight*. His fight with Audrea weighed on his mind, as he met the director in the middle of the arena. "Hi, John."

Waters nodded, his gaze locked on the script in his hands. "We got the horses you wanted. There all roans, and none of them has ever been ridden."

"Okay, good. I thought we'd start with some footage of me riding them while they buck. If one stops bucking, I'll keep switching horses till we get enough. And, uh, where are the panels I asked for?"

"I decided to go a different way on that, Yak. I want to shoot the entire arena."

"But you don't understand. If you set the panels in a V shape just off camera, the horse will go where we want him to go for the stunt. He has to throw me over the fence into the brass band."

"Yes, I know the scene, but I want a wider shot. You're a cowboy. Just ride the horse over there."

"Come on, John. These are wild horses. They buck and run wherever they want to. You can't control where they go until they're broken."

Waters looked up and said, "I'm the director, not you, and we're shooting the wide view. Just do your job, will you?" Before Yak could say anymore, Waters walked away, shouting instructions to a cameraman. This was not what he had expected, and Yak certainly was not going to be on his way home in half an hour. But with his third child on the way, this was not the time to lose a job. He rode three horses for the bucking scenes and held the fourth for the stunt. He talked to it as he tossed the saddle on. "Well, you're a big boy. I think I'll call you Titan. Give me a good, hard ride over

143

there, fella, and try not to do anything crazy." He climbed aboard and nodded to Waters. "Okay, John, let's do it."

Cameras rolled, and Yak pulled away from the snubbing horse. He wasn't sure how he'd control a bucking horse well enough to ride him to a specific spot, but that wasn't his biggest worry. Titan squealed and spun. "Oh, boy, this ain't good." He reared onto his hind legs, and Yak thought that would be great for the cameras, but then Titan fell over backwards. He landed squarely on Yak's chest, driving the saddle horn into his stomach. Barely conscious, Yak couldn't breathe, and then he realized the horse was still on him, balanced with his hoofs skyward. Yak thought he would die, but Titan rolled off him, and then his world went black.

* * *

The first thing he saw at the hospital was Audrea's face, and the first thing he felt was a stabbing in his gut. Then came her voice. "Doctor, he's conscious. Can I talk to him?"

"Make it quick. The gurney is on its way."

"Can you hear me, baby?"

His pain was so severe he could hardly speak. "Are the boys okay?"

"They're with the neighbors."

"How bad am I hurt?"

"Don't worry about that. They're taking you into surgery in a few minutes, but the doctor says he knows what to do. You're going to be fine. Really, it's going to be fine." Her voice faltered and a tear found her eye. "I'm so sorry I was mean to you."

"How is John?"

"John Waters? He's sitting in the hall crying. He blames himself for this. He said, if he'd listened to you, it never would've happened."

"Tell him not to blame himself. I don't blame him."

Audrea started to speak, but someone pulled her away, and a man's voice said, "It's time to go, Mr. Canutt." And, he blacked out again.

Yakima woke to the sound of Audrea's voice, but he wasn't sure what she was saying. The room seemed strange, like looking out of the bottom of a bottle. "Is it over?" he asked.

"Yes, thank God. It felt like the longest time while you were in there."

"Well, I guess I won't be leaving you just yet."

"I was afraid you might be."

"What do you mean?"

"You're going to think I'm crazy, but this is absolutely true. I saw you about the time of your accident, at least I saw something that looked like you. You were smiling, the happiest I'd ever seen you. It scared the daylights out of me. I thought you were dead, and I prayed, 'Oh, dear God, don't do this. Don't take him yet.' Then the image disappeared. I called the studio, and they told me you were on your way here."

"I guess your prayer must've gotten through, because I'm still here and ticking like a watch." A pain shot through his gut. "Oh, that hurts. So, did the doctor tell you how much damage there is? Did he say when I can go back to work?"

"You banged up your intestines, your diaphragm, one kidney, and some other organs, but I'm not sure what they are. You're lucky to be alive, Yak."

"What about my work? Come on, I need to know."

"He said you'd be crazy to go back to stunting again."

Yakima took a moment to think about what the doctor had said, then he grinned and said, "He doesn't know what a good nurse I have."

* * *

The stay in the hospital lasted but a few days, and Audrea took him home. She nursed him for a week with occasional doses of laudanum, until the pain reached the level where he could bear it. When he was able to stand, he started walking on crutches and stretching. At the end of the second week, he made his way to the dinner table unassisted, his waist still bound with bandages. He looked at the two chickens and bowls of vegetables and said, "That's a lot of food for the four of us."

"We're having company for dinner."

"Company? Who?"

Before she could answer, Tap ran into the room. "Mama, Uncle John is here."

"That's fine, son. Tell him to come on in."

As he entered the dining room, Wayne stopped and said, "I hope you don't mind, Audrea, but I brought somebody with me."

"Oh, not at all. Bring him right in."

Yak smiled, as the young man walked in. "My gosh, Tim. I haven't seen you since *Stagecoach*. Sweetheart, this is the man of your dreams, Tim Holt." Audrea blushed and motioned for them to sit. "It's good to see you guys."

"John told me about your accident, and he said you wouldn't mind if we dropped in to check on you."

"Come anytime. You guys don't need to ask."
His signature dimples shone, as Holt smiled. "Thanks, Yak. So, how are you getting along."

"Good, really good. I don't expect to be laid up much longer."

"That's great news. I, uh, I do have a favor I wanted to ask."

"Fire away."

"RKO is talking to me about a starring role, maybe even a series of movies. Now, you know I can ride, but I think it would help my chances of getting the role, if I could do a couple of tricks, like that scissors mount you do. That might seal the deal for me."

"You can't do that trick?"

Holt's expression fell. "No? Well, I just thought . . ."
"It's not that I don't want you to do it. You're not tall enough, not without a platform to jump from, and

147

you'd have to keep that off camera. You'd do better with a running mount, what we call a pony express, and I can teach you that in ten minutes."

"That would be great. I can't tell you how much I'd appreciate that."

Audrea didn't appear as sure. "Hold on, guys. My husband has a way to go before he's well enough for that kind of thing."

"Don't worry," Wayne answered. "I'll keep an eye on him, and I can help too. Shoot, Yak's the one who taught me how to do that mount." He shook a cigarette from the pack. "Do you mind if I smoke?"

Audrea nodded her consent, and he offered one to Yak. "No thanks, John. I'm not all the way back with my breathing yet, but I'm close."

"Well, let me know when you are, because we need a little advice for a stunt in a movie we're shooting." It was exactly what Yakima wanted to hear. "What movie?"

"It's called *Dark Command*, and there's this scene where Gabby and I are being chased by some raiders. Do you remember that big bluff at Sherwood Lake?" Yak nodded. "Well, we drive a team of horses and a wagon off it into the water. I told them you're the only guy I trust to direct that scene."

"How soon do you need it?"

"Two or three weeks from now. Do you think you'd be up to it?"

"No question about it. In fact, I'll probably be ready to do the jump myself by then."

"Oh, no you won't." Audrea snapped. "I nearly lost you on the last stunt you tried. It's time for you to find a safer kind of work."

Yak lowered his gaze, winked at Wayne, and said, "Maybe you're right. Let's take care of this chicken before it gets cold. And, tomorrow I'll start looking for a new job, maybe a librarian or something."

* * *

He covered his mouth as he spoke into the telephone. "Yes, I'll be there on time, John. Did they finish the ramp?"

"All done. Does Audrea know you're going to do this gag?"

"No, and please don't tell her. She treats me like a crystal glass, but I'm okay and we could use the extra money. This new house isn't going to pay for itself."

"Did you ever tell her you were the one who asked me to bring Tim to dinner that night?"

"Are you kidding? Look, I've got to go. I think I hear her coming." He eased the receiver onto its hook, but Audrea wasn't fooled.

"Who are you talking to?"

"Uh, just the studio. I wanted to make sure they set up the stunt the way I told them to."

"Why don't you just go out there and see?"

"Go to the set? Well, yeah, that's the best thing to do, but I thought you wanted me to take you shopping."

"I don't need you for that. Mama and I can do it."

"Okay, I'll just take a ride out there to, you know, look things over."

"You do that, and take Tap with you."

Now he knew she wasn't fooled. Tap was her informant, the one who would surely tell her, if he dared attempt the stunt, but he had no good way out of it. "Come on, boy. Get in the car."

They took Highway 101 from North Hollywood and drove the sixty miles to a pristine lake that lay among the Santa Monica Mountains. Yak tried to talk about baseball, but Tap was unusually quiet. He seemed to know exactly what his job was, as if coached by an insistent mother. "Say, son, I was wondering what you think you might want for Christmas this year."

"Christmas? That's a long way off."

"I know, but maybe we could get you something early, something you'd really like."

"You don't want me to tell on you, if you do something dangerous today, do you?"

"It's not that, well, it's kind of that. Your mother means well, but I'm completely healed, and this is what I do for a living. You know I never got to high school, and men like me have to do what they have to do."

"Mama says you have adhesions. What does that mean?"

"It means some of the stuff the doctor sewed together inside me is sticking to other stuff, but it'll pull loose sometime. I think that's kinda normal with surgery." Tap stared out the window, and Yak changed his tune. "Look, this is the way it's going to be. I'm going to make that jump today, and you are not going to tell your mother. Is that clear?" No answer. "Did you hear me, boy?"

"I heard, but what is it worth to you?"

"What are you looking for, son?"

"A horse."

"Where would you ride it?"

"There's not a house within half a mile of ours. We've got plenty of room for me to ride."

"Well, I'd think about that. Now, you'd have to raise the money for your own saddle."

"I've already done that." Then Yak heard a voice that sounded like his own echoing back to him. "Have we got a deal, partner?"

"You're quite the negotiator, aren't you? That's okay, but I want one other condition. You go to college."

"I don't need to go to college, Daddy. I'm going to be a stuntman, like you."

"Hold the phone on that. I do stunts because I have to. Your mother and I want something better for you and Joe. We want you to have choices. Be a doctor or

151

something. Then you could set other people's bones instead of having them set yours." Again, the car was bathed in silence. "How bad do you want that horse?"

"I'll go to college, but I'm still going to be a stuntman."

"That's all I need to hear, son. Maybe when you go to college, they'll teach you to have better sense than your old man has."

The security guard checked his identification, and Yak drove to a copse of trees near the bluff. Sol Siegel met him as he stepped out of his car. "I looked over your equipment, Yak, and I've never seen so many trip wires and latches, but how are you going to get those horses to jump off the cliff?"

"We put blinders on them, Sol, and we paint them to look like their eyes. That way the camera won't see the difference. I've rigged a special wagon, so the horses will be free before we hit the water. It's going to be great."

"It had better be. I've got five thousand dollars invested in it."

"Don't worry. Now, I need to double check the setup." He walked to the edge of the bluff, with Tap close behind, and inspected the ramp. "Hey, you guys throw some more dirt over there. If I can see the wood, the camera can see it. We want this to look like it's natural." As the crew started work, he went back to the car and opened the trunk.

"So, that's where you hid your cowboy clothes." Tap said. "Mama looked all over the house for them. She was going to throw them out."

"That's what I figured." He changed shirts and pulled on his cowboy hat. He started to tell Tap to stay with the car, but decided to put him next to one of the cameras. "So, you think you want to do stunts, huh? Well, you stand here. Maybe it won't look so glamourous after you seen how it's done." At the call of action, a buckboard pulled by a team of horses raced toward them. As it neared the precipice, John Wayne pulled the horses to a stop, and Yakima climbed into his place. He nodded to the director and whipped the team into a gallop. When they reached the end of the ramp, he pulled the cable to release the wagon from the team, and they all went airborne. Yak leaped to the left and cleared the wagon, but he hit the water like hitting a wall. It felt like every adhesion and every tendon pulled loose at the same time. He managed to hold his breath until he surfaced, then grabbed a horse's harness, and let it swim him to shore. He knew he'd done the stunt too early, but he was alive.

The other stuntmen helped him back up the hill, and he found Tap waiting for him. There was no hiding the pain, not even from the boy who might tell on him. "Help me to the car, son. I need to lay down for a while." He hobbled across the set, dripping wet, and said, "Well, Tap, there it is, and here's your father,

153

having to be helped to his car. I don't guess you want any more to do with this business."

Tap took a long breath and let it out slowly. "It's the greatest thing I've ever seen. I want everything to do with this business."

Yak wagged his head and looked at his producer. "Well, what did you think?"

"That was outstanding, and I'm willing to spend another five grand, if you can come up with a second gag that good."

"I'll work on it."

"Say, Yak, have you ever thought about directing action sequences?"

"It's been my dream for ten years. I'm getting too old to jump out of falling wagons."

"Good. Then we'll work out the details for my next movie."

Siegel walked away, and Yak wrapped his arm around Tap's shoulders. "Hey, there's some good news. Maybe your old man won't have to break his neck after all."

Chapter Seven

Joe's voice resonated through the house, as he ran down the hall yelling, "Mama, Mama, there's a strange man in your bedroom." Yakima stood in front of the mirror, dressed in a light blue outfit, white hat, and black mask. He saw the image of Audrea in the doorway behind him with Joe clinging to her skirt.

"What in the world are you wearing?" she asked.

"It's that new movie I told you about."

"Are you playing the Lone Ranger?"

"No, Lee Powell has that part. I'm going to double him for a few stunts."

"I thought you were going to direct the action in that movie. Your hip isn't well yet, and don't try to tell me it is. I've seen you limping, when you thought I wasn't looking."

He pulled the mask off, sat on the edge of the bed, and called his son to him. "See, it's just me, buddy. Your mama thinks I'm going to hurt myself again, but I'm not." He looked up to Audrea. "There are no big gags in this one. They don't have the budget for that. I'll rig a couple of stagecoaches to flip, do some horse tricks, and throw a few punches with the bad guys. That's all. I didn't see a reason to hire a stuntman, when I can do these gags and make the extra money."

"But you're a lot taller than Lee Powell. Who's going to believe it's him?"

"Everybody, I hope. When he puts on the mask, things change, even his voice. If you think people won't believe he's doing the gags, just wait till they hear the voiceover. It's bad. Oh, by the way, I met a man from Australia, a guy named McCall. He wants me to round up some cowboys for a rodeo he's putting on down there."

"Yak, you are absolutely not bulldogging again."

"No, no. I'll recruit the guys who do that, and I'll do a few basic stunts for them, you know, fancy mounts and the like. Well, I might ride a couple of broncs, you know, just to keep a hand in. And, you and the kids can come. It'll be great. And, John tells me he's shooting a war movie about a girl who escapes from the Nazis to Montana. I'd get to direct the action scenes for that, and it means doing something other than strictly westerns. This could be a career-changer."

"You're trying to get me to think about something other than these stunts you're going to do, aren't you?" She stroked the side of his face and said, "You just be sure to come home in the same shape you leave."

Audrea left the room, but Joe stayed. "Those guys in the movies aren't real cowboys, are they, Dad?"

"Well, they're actors, but some of them are pretty good on a horse."

"You're a real cowboy. Tap told me so."

156

"I used to be, but I haven't ridden in a rodeo for quite a while now."

"Daddy, who's the best cowboy you ever saw?"

"I assume you mean other than me, because I was the best cowboy. I don't mean to sound proud, son, but it's just the truth. Now, the second-best cowboy would've been Jackson Sundown. He was a full-blooded Nez Perce. I met him when he was about fifty years old, but he was still a riding fool. I learned a lot from him."

"Who was the best horse?"

"Tipperary, no question about it. He was the finest animal I ever saw. Nobody else has ever ridden him, and I rode him twice. He was strong, fast, and just plain beautiful."

For no reason known to Yak, Joe changed the subject. "Tap jumped off the house today."

"Are you tattling on your brother again? Jumped off the house? So, that's why we had those leaks. I had to pay fifteen hundred dollars to get those tiles fixed."

"Yeah, he was jumping onto some old mattresses."

"That boy will be the death of me. I've told him and told him, but he just won't stop." He set Joe down from the bed. "You go find your brother and tell him the Lone Ranger wants to see him."

Joe said, "Okay" and scampered off.

Yak slipped his mask back on and muttered, "I'll teach that boy what 'Hi-yo Silver' is all about."

* * *

Before leaving for the Land Down Under, Yak squeezed in a movie with John Wayne, *Three Faces West*. But, even as action ramrod, he still performed stunts. He told himself there were few other stuntmen with the body type to double Wayne, but he knew it was simply hard to give up stunting. Directing was a dream, maybe a dream that would never come true. And, stunts still paid the bills.

He sat in a deckchair, clad in only a pair of swim trunks, watching Audrea with the children at the pool. They had been married over ten years, and all he did was to love her more. He draped a towel around his shoulders, walked across the deck, and sat next to her with his feet in the water. "Is the trip going okay for you?"

"Yes, I'm glad we came. It's been so peaceful. I was a little afraid at first."

"Well, they don't normally get bad storms this time of year."

"I wasn't so much worried about storms. Europe is at war again, and I was afraid a German U-boat might mistake us for a supply ship or something."

"Don't let that bother you. You know, when I was in the Navy, I learned how to navigate by the stars, and we're way too far south for U-boats." He couldn't hold back a half grin. "One good thing is that you'll get to see me ride for the first time."

"Yes, and I'm not sure what to make of that. The only horse riding I've seen you do has been in those movies."

"You saw me ride Rex down that mountain side in *The Devil Horse*. That's about as close as it gets to the real thing. I don't reckon the Aussies will have a horse that holds a candle to Rex. I think we'll all make good rides, but I'm kind of worried about the other guys."

"Why? They're all good cowboys, aren't they?"

"Oh, yeah, every one of them. That's why I picked them, when Mr. McCall asked me to put this show together. But I talked to a couple of them yesterday, and they don't have contracts."

"Why would they travel half way around the world to do a show without a contract?"

"McCall offered them a lot of money to come, and they're afraid to offend him. You've got to remember, they have families too, and they're not in the movie business. These guys can't afford to lose a job like this. I mean, we all get to compete in the rodeo events and win money, and my five thousand is guaranteed no matter what, but these boys don't have any kind of guarantee."

"Do you think Mr. McCall would cheat them out of their money?"

"I hope not, but it happens, and it's not just him. There are other people involved in promoting this show."

"What if they refuse to pay and point at each other?"

"What do you do when one of the boys breaks a lamp and both deny they did it?"

"I spank them both to be sure I get the guilty one."

"Well, that's what I'd do too." He shook his head and chuckled.

"What's so funny?"

"Not so much funny as weird. I made a movie once about this very thing, in fact I made two of them. The first was *Man from Utah* with John, and a few years later we shot one with Tex Ritter with exactly the same plot. I even played the same character. Crazy stuff, but they paid me for both movies. Now, I know those were just stories, but I've seen it happen at rodeos. They pay off ten cents on the dollar, or nothing at all."

She handed him the baby and said, "Here, why don't you take Honey for a walk around the ship. It'll make you feel better."

He took the infant in his arms and rose to his feet. "Well, baby girl, let's go walking, before the kangaroos get us both."

* * *

The ship landed in Melbourne under bright skies. Yakima had scarcely disembarked, when a man called his name. "Why, it's Yakima Canutt." He shook his hand like an old friend. "It's so good to see you." Then the man left as quickly as he came.

"Audrea, did you see that?"

"Sure. I guess they're just really friendly down here. Oh, there's our ride."

They stood aside, as porters loaded their luggage into the trunk of a Pontiac, and another man approached them. "Are you Yakima?"

"Yes, sir. Do I know you?"

"No, you don't know me, Mate, but you just earned me twenty shillings."

He turned to Audrea. "Okay, I get it now. I heard they were going to run some kind of promotion for the show. This must be a contest to see how many people can recognize me before the rodeo starts. Let's get to the hotel. I think we're supposed to host a big, swanky party tonight."

* * *

He could hardly keep his eyes off her, as Yak escorted Audrea into the hotel conference room. Her figure was as trim as the day he met her, and the satin evening gown hugged each detail. The room teemed with local celebrities and public officials, but he picked out a familiar face. "Mr. McCall, I'd like you to meet my wife. This is Audrea."

He plucked the glasses from his round nose, and offered his right hand. "How do you do, Mrs. Canutt? It is my great pleasure to meet you."

"And, mine to meet you, sir."

"Your husband is causing quite a stir in our town. The Australian Stampede will be the biggest show ever to hit Melbourne. We are very excited."

161

"That's great to hear. Yak and I are just as excited about seeing your beautiful country."

"Tell me, Mr. Canutt, what was the most enjoyable part of your trip so far?"

"Pago Pago."

"Really? I thought you might have said our zoo."

"Well, we ain't been there yet. We're taking the kids tomorrow, but Pago Pago was beautiful, very green. Then we went to Suva, and they have brahmas, so that made me feel at home?"

"Brahmas?"

"Yeah, brahma bulls. You know, big ugly steers with a hump on their shoulders."

"Ah, it sounds like our Charbray. It's the most repulsive breed of cattle I've ever seen. You'll see a couple of those in the bulldogging contest."

"Yak won't be bulldogging," Audrea interrupted.

"Well, that's a shame. That event does pay well, and our audience will be disappointed not to see him in it."

Yak took her by the arm and said, "Why don't we get something to drink?" They walked away, and he looked back at McCall with a nod of the head and a wink.

Both of the Canutts were happy when the party was over and they could get back to their room and their children. The long trip by boat had given them time to adjust to the dramatic time change, so they slept well. When the morning came, Audrea and one of their hosts took the children to the zoo, while Yak spent his

162

day at the arena. "Now, I'm going to need a couple of straps bolted to the bottom of the wagon tongue"

"Down there?" one of the crewmen asked.

"Yes, right there and there. And, I want a metal bar on the back of the stage. Do you see where I'm pointing?" They both nodded. "One of my men will dress as the bad guy and drive the stage. I don't mean any disrespect to you guys, but I'm the one doing the trick, and I know my men." He rubbed the back of his neck.

"Are you hurt?"

"No, I took a bad fall in a movie a couple of weeks ago. I flipped off the back of a horse, you know?" They shook their heads. "Okay, it's a stunt. Anyway, I landed wrong and hurt my neck, but the studio doctor said I was all right. He told me to keep my neck stiff when I do any horse riding." He could see by the look on their faces, they were only interested in getting their jobs done. "Let me know when you finish. I want to double check everything."

A voice called to him from the ticket office. "Mr. Canutt, we have a call for you."

"A call for me? Are you sure?" He hurried to the phone and held the receiver to his ear. "This is Yakima Canutt. Who am I talking to?"

"It's Audrea."

"What's wrong, baby?"

"We just had a terrible day at the zoo. A koala bear scratched my chin, and some bird tried to eat Tap's finger. The baby's been crying her head off, and I wish I were home."

"Are the hostesses there with you?"

"Yes, two of them."

"Then let them keep the kids, and you come to the show tonight."

"How can I do that when my children are so upset?"

"Maybe that's why you should. Come on, you've never seen me ride, not in a rodeo. I'm going to show these young guys how it's done. The kids will be all right. Grab your purse and come. You'll have a good time. I promise."

"Well, I'll think about it."

He knew that meant yes. "Great. I'll meet you at the gate at seven."

* * *

The arena was filled with screaming fans for the opening day of the week-long rodeo, even though the first day was reserved for entertainment, not competition. Indians danced in tribal fare and Yakima performed his famous gag from *Stagecoach*. He slid under the stage, climbed up the back, and overpowered the outlaw. The crowd cheered when he returned to the arena and climbed the chute for an exhibition bronc ride. He looked down at the horse and said, "Wait a minute. That's an English saddle, and I'm not even wearing spurs. How am I supposed to ride with that?" The only answer was the cheers from the paying customers, and he knew he couldn't back out.

They were barely out of the gate, when Yak felt his neck pop and his arms go numb. On the second buck he fell hard to the ground. The stands roared with laughter, and he gave them a wave, but he wasn't laughing. It was the first time Audrea had seen him ride, and he lay in the dirt. He marched out of the arena fuming and growled, "Somebody give me a set of spurs."

Once properly shod, he returned to the chutes to a smattering of boos. He picked the best of their horses and climbed aboard. And, he gave them the ride they had come to see, the ride he wanted Audrea to see. He spent the next three nights bronc busting and bulldogging, in spite of her asking him not to, and he was poised to win top money. Then the bottom fell out, literally. It rained for four days, and the rodeo was cancelled. When the word reached Audrea, she told Yak, and he took his contract to the head of the Wild Australian Stampede. "Mr. Plum, Stuart McCall tells me you're the man in charge for paying people off from the rodeo."

He looked up from his desk and wiped a cloth over his pale face. "I'm the man in charge, but as to paying off, well, there is no money to pay off. You saw it yourself. We were rained out."

Yak laid his contract in front of him. "Is that your signature?"

Plum looked it over carefully and said, "That is my signature, sir, and may I say, Mr. Canutt, that you are a shrewd businessman. I will pay the money we promised." He wrote a check for Yak's five-thousand-dollar guarantee. "I think our business is finished, but perhaps I could ask you about something."

"Fire away."

"Some of my people say that man, that Indian, they call him Iron Eyes Cody. They tell me I should hire some security people, that he might cut my scalp off. Is that true?"

"Let me tell you about Iron Eyes Cody. He plays Indians in movies, yeah, but he was born in Louisiana. He's a good man, but he ain't an Indian. His father is from Italy and I think his mother is from Sicily. He won't be scalping anybody. But those other boys, well, you might want to find a way to settle with them. They're a rough crowd."

"Would you be willing to talk with them, reason with them."

"I can try, but my family and I are taking a plane to New Zealand in the morning to catch a ship home. Once we're gone, you're on your own." He stuffed his check into his pocket and took the elevator to the ground floor, where he found five of his friends. "Where are you headed, boys?"

Perry Ivory stood tall and lean with a stern expression that almost always covered his face. He pulled his hat back and said, "We're fixing to go up there and get our money."

"That's gonna be hard to do. He says he ain't got any money."

"Did you get paid, Yak?"

"You know I did. I had a contract, just like I tried to get you to do. He had to pay me."

"Well, he's gonna pay us too, or we'll take it out of his hide."

"I reckon that your business, but think about it. Do you want the morning papers to tell about a bunch of ragtag Americans who came to Australia and don't know how to behave? This ain't the first show that's been rained out and it won't be the last." He took Ivory's hat from his head, dusted off some imaginary dust, and put it back. "Now, you boys came half way around the world, because I asked you to. And, you've got a right to be mad, but you ain't going up there and whip that old man's butt. You'll have to whip mine first."

"We didn't come here to fight with you, Yak, but we ain't even got the money to get back home."

"All right, I see your problem. You, and I mean you, Perry, not the rest. You go up there and talk to him. See if he'll get you home. If he says he can't, then I'll pay your way home myself."

"That's fair enough." Ivory stepped onto the elevator and looked back. "But I'll tell you this. I ain't never leaving the good old USA again."

* * *

Audrea stood at her new ironing board in the kitchen, pressing shirts, and she called to her husband in the den. "Yak, would you turn that radio up?"

He looked down at the cast on one ankle and the splint on the other, and said, "Tap, turn the radio up for you mama." The youngster put his dime novel down and turned the nob on their Philco model 40. "Is that Roy Rogers singing?"

"Yes, it's his new record. I just love to hear his voice."

"Yeah, he's good, but you know I got these broken ankles doubling for him."

"That's not his fault, Yak."

Tap sat back down and asked, "Did you get to ride Trigger?"

"That was the best part of the movie, son. In fact, I had been riding him when I got hurt." Tap didn't ask how the accident happened, but Yak told him anyway. "You see, I rode up behind this panel truck with bandits in it, trying to get away. I jumped from Trigger onto the back of the truck. That all went fine. Then we shot a stunt where I jump from a wagon. I've done that over and over. Well, I don't know if they were driving too fast or what happened, but I landed wrong. Broke both ankles, and the sad part is they cut that scene from the movie. I busted my legs for nothing."

"Did it hurt bad?"

"Like sin. I got sick on my stomach, started puking everywhere." He relit his pipe and let his story sink in.

168

"That's the way it is with stuntmen. Sometimes, you get busted up like this. I'm going to get out of doing stunts soon. Smart people never start it."

Tap took his book and left the room, as Audrea walked in with three cowboy shirts on hangers. "I'll put these in your closet. I don't guess you'll need them for a while."

"Maybe. Republic called me about working on a film with Errol Flynn, but it doesn't start production for another month or six weeks. I expect to be well by then."

"If you say so. I swear, I've just given up on you ever getting out of the stuntman game. So, what do you plan to do with yourself in the meantime?"

"I've been thinking about that, and I can't sit here and do nothing. I'd like to go home."

"Home? You are home."

Yeah, I know, but I mean to the ranch, to see my mother and Alex. We haven't been in a long time, and the kids would love it there."

"Let me think about that. You know, the last time we went, she was a little cool to me."

"Oh, that's just her way. She's crazy about you. Come on, what do you say?"

"Well, maybe we should get away. I heard something on the radio while you were in the bathroom. They said Japan attacked our naval base in Hawaii yesterday."

"Pearl Harbor? My God, we were just there a few weeks ago. Why would they want to do that?"

"They didn't say why, but President Roosevelt has asked for a declaration of war."

"That's not good. I mean, what else could he do? I saw a lot of good men die in horrible ways when we fought Germany. I hope they get it over before our two boys come of age."

* * *

The orchards were bare of fruit in the heart of winter, the ground covered with a dusting of snow, but Yakima and his mother still liked to sit on the porch and read. They said little until she asked about his legs. "Are you having much trouble with that cast, son?"

"I wasn't at first, but now I'm getting some burrs and foxtail stickers in it. Do you see that little bit of blood? Well, all this stuff is driving me crazy."

"Why don't you cut it off?"

"I've thought about it, but the doctor said I need to keep it another couple of weeks. The studio said I was to check with them first." He looked across the ranch, the corrals and storehouses he helped build, a small herd of horses in the pasture, and he breathed it all in. "Sometimes, I really miss this place."

"Well, you wouldn't know it be how often you come to visit."

He didn't even try to explain his schedule. "Where's Alex?"

"He drove over to Seattle again. He says he wants to go fight the Japs, but the Army recruiter says he's too old to join. He's tried to enlist five or six times, and they always tell him the same. Of course, he's got those other problems."

"Yeah, I'm worried about this war. They say we're going to fight Germany again too. I don't understand that. We whipped them good twenty years ago and then let them rebuild their army. I hear they marched through Poland in just days." He ran his hand down the arm of the rocker and said, "This is gonna sound selfish, but I sure hope it doesn't hurt the movie business again. I need the work."

"Alex goes to see every one of your pictures. I don't get out much, but he goes."

"They tell me I'll get to write the action scenes in the next one. It's another John Wayne movie."

"I just love that John Wayne. He's so big and handsome. When he jumped down on those horses in that one movie, lands sake, it scared me to death. I thought he'd killed himself for sure."

"That wasn't John, Mama, that was me."

"No, I'm talking about that stagecoach thing. I saw him."

"Yeah, I know, but they make it look like, well, never mind. I'm glad he didn't get hurt too."

"What's that book you're reading, son?"
"It's about handling explosives. I got some training when I served on that mine sweeper during the war,

but I thought I should brush up on it. I've got to blow up about twenty wagons in this next picture, and I'd rather not make a mistake on that. By the way, is it all right if I take the boys riding tomorrow? Tap is getting to be quite a horseman, and I'll keep Joe with me."

"Just be careful of that mare. I think she might be in season. Speaking of mares, is that gal of yours planning to have any more babies?"

"I don't know. We didn't exactly plan these three."

"Maybe you ought to get some of that stuff they give guys in the Army."

"Oh, boy, now it's really getting uncomfortable."

"What's that you say, son?"

"I said, 'it's always good talking to you, Mama.' I think I'll go in the house and see how Audrea's doing with supper."

* * *

Yak rode a train to Kanab, Utah and, from there, took a cab to the set of *In Old Oklahoma*. It was good to be back on the job, but his right leg was still bound in the cast, and it was more painful than ever. He hobbled over to the prop wagon and got a pair of snips. He cut away the case, and an acrid odor rose from it. "Take a look at that, John."

"I'm not sure I want to with that odor," Wayne answered.

"Yeah, I know. If I'd left it on another week, I think it would've gone gangrene. That's the thing about doctors. They'll mess you up if you don't watch it."

"You don't look well enough to be doing stunts to me. I could ask Joe Kane to get somebody, if you're not ready."

"I'm ready. Give me time to wash that foot, kind of get the stench out, and I'll be good." He soaked his foot in a bucket of water for a few minutes and then someone dropped a pair of boots beside him. "Were you planning to do these stunts in your bare feet, Yak?"

"Thanks, John. Here, sit down. Tell me about the family."

Wayne sat on an inverted bucket and said, "Not good. You know Josie and I have been having our problems. Well, she moved out. It looks like it over for us."

"I hate to hear that. You guys have been married for a long time."

"Yeah, over ten years, but I was a kid when we got married, like you were the first time."

"Boy, I hope this goes better for you than it did for me. I had to join the Navy to get away from her."

"I tried to join the Army, but the studio said they'd sue me for breach of contract, if I did."

"You're too old for that, John."

"Errol Flynn joined up, and he's older than me. I even applied to the OSS. Come to find out, they accepted me for the Field Photographic Unit, but Josie hid the letter."

"What is the OSS?"

"Spy stuff. I think you infiltrate Germany and get pictures of military installations and things like that. Anyway, it's too late for that now."

Yak didn't know quite what to say, but he wanted to encourage his best friend. "You know, I was in a serial last year about spies."

"I saw part of it, *Spy Smasher*. I don't mean to hurt your feelings, Yak, but that thing was awful. I mean, some guy running around in a leather flight cap and goggles, wearing a cape. What kind of disguise is that?"

"I didn't say I wrote it. I just did the stunts. And, yes, the outfit felt kind of silly, but they paid me well. How do you like the plot of this movie?"

"I like it a lot, and you're going to like the way it ends. My character is trying to get a bunch of wagons loaded with oil to a refinery before it closes, so he can claim a contract. The bad guy, who really isn't so bad, plants dynamite in some of the wagons. It sounds like a wing dinger."

* * *

In a week's time, Yak was well enough to direct the closing stunts of the film. Forty-five Conestoga wagons and buckboards sat strewn across the open plains, ready to charge full-speed between camera trucks. The director lit a cigarette and said, "I know it's a little

174

late to ask this, Yak, but are you sure you can pull this trick off?"

"Absolutely."

"Okay, are you ready to go?"

"We're ready, Al, but I'm going to drive the lead wagon. If, somehow, I got those charges wrong, I don't want someone else to pay the price for it."

"You're starting to make me a nervous."

"No, no, it's okay. The charges are the same on each wagon we plan to wreck. Once mine goes off, and we see it works, then we can start setting off the other charges. It's going to be fine. You'll love it."

"I hope so. It's certainly big enough, and costs enough money. John, we're going to pick you up in some wide shots, but be sure you stay clear of those exploding wagons. With all due respect, if someone's going to get blown up out here, don't let it be my star."

Wayne pulled his horse around and said, "Don't worry about me, Al. I'll take care of myself."

Yak climbed aboard, Rogell gave the call for action, and the massive stunt began. As the team of horses came to a trot, Yak started to question himself, but he was nearing the end of the trip cable. If he were to stop, it had to be now. But there would be no stopping. He heard the cable pop, as it freed the horses and twisted the wagon's front wheels. Yak yanked on a cord, as he leapt from the seat, and a series of explosions blew the back of the wagon into flames and sent it tumbling. He rolled over the ground and, once he stopped, he motioned to Rogell to keep rolling. Time after time wagons exploded, rolling over, and spilling tanks of oil onto the ground. Flames rose in every direction, swept by the prairie winds. The herd of wagons and camera trucks ran past Yak, covering him with dust in their wake. He pulled himself to one knee and watched the biggest gag he'd ever designed. It was beautiful, epic. When it was over, John Wayne rode to his side and stepped down from his horse. "Well, Yak," he said. "That's the most spectacular stunt I've ever seen, bar none. You've told me for years you want to be an action director. I don't see how anyone could deny you that now."

Chapter Eight

Audrea sat at her dresser, brushing her hair, while Yakima read a script in bed and wrote on a notepad. The war raged in Europe and the Pacific, and she worried about how long it would have to last before the Army started looking for older men. But, for now, they lived in peace, her husband had enough work to provide a good living for their family, and their love was yet to fade. What more could she ask for? She laid the brush aside and turned to face the bed. "Are you mad about something?"

"No," he answered. "I'm just frustrated. We're almost ready to shoot the last battle scene for this movie, and Breezy won't listen to a thing I say."

"Is he the action director?"

"Yeah, second unit director, and a lush. I've worked with him before, but it's never been this bad. This scene has hundreds of men and horses, and he wants my stuntmen to take falls right in the middle of all that. We never have people fall in front of running horses. It's always to the side. Anybody knows that."

"Did you talk to Mr. Walsh about it?"

"Well, I don't like going around Breezy, but I had to, and all I got was, 'Don't worry about it, Yak. Breezy directed the action in Ben Hur. He knows what to do.' Like I don't know he did Ben Hur, but that was fifteen years ago. Breezy Eason has been through a lot of whiskey since then. Do you know how he got the name Breezy? Well, I'll tell you. It's because he's so breezy with safety on the set. A stuntman gets busted up or a horse gets killed, and he just calls for another one."

She slipped from her bench to the edge of the bed and ran her lean fingers through his hair. "Why don't you put it away for tonight. Things will be clearer in the morning."

"Ahh, I guess you're right. I kind of feel sorry for the guy. You know, his little boy was hit and killed by a truck years ago. Maybe that's what started him drinking so much, but that doesn't give him the right to take so many risks with other people's lives. We're going to have an understanding tomorrow, or I may be home early.

* * *

Breezy Eason stood next to a camera truck, his trouser legs tucked inside his knee-high boots, and a light gage in his hand. He wasn't as tall as Yak, but still a big man, and yet one that looked worn beyond his fifty-five years. He scratched his bearded chin and stared at Yak from beneath heavy eyebrows. "Where have you been, Canutt? Don't you know we start early?"

"Well, I know where I wasn't."

"And, where would that be?"

"Pulling you out of some bar last night. Wait a minute. I shouldn't have said that. I'm upset about the

178

way you want to shoot this scene, but I know better than to take cheap shots."

"Upset? Why would you be upset? We've covered every angle."

"Let me give you a couple of examples." He opened the script and held it out for Eason to see. "Look here. You've got one of the Indians being dragged by a horse. Now, that's okay, we do it all the time, but the other horses are too close. The stuntman could get trampled."

"That's why we call them stuntmen, and they're well paid to take those chances. You ought to know that."

"Then there's this charge. Custer's men are huddled in tight formation, and the Sioux drive their horses into the circle. I'm not saying we cut the scene. In fact, I like it. The problem is the camera angle. Mr. Walsh told me you talked him into filming this as one, continuous shot. A couple of quick changes in camera, and we get the same effect without hurting anyone. Don't you think that would be better. I know you don't want anyone hurt. I'm only asking that you think about it."

Eason checked his light gage, as if in deep thought. Then he said, "Okay, I thought about it, and the answer is no. You tell your stuntmen to do their jobs and let me worry about directing."

"No. I won't do it."

"Well, you can always complain to the director. But,I can tell you I already got his approval, so go knock yourself out."

Yak stepped closer and took Eason's shirt in his fist. "I won't be going to anybody. You either change the scene, or I'm going to beat you senseless, right here and right now."

"Take your hands off me. You ain't gonna do nothing."

"Yak shoved him to the ground and knelt over his prone body with one knee on his chest. "I ain't playing with you, Breezy. How many times have I covered for you, because you were drunk on the job? How many times have I shown the crew what to do, because you were passed out in your trailer?"

"I'll have your job for this."

Yak slapped him hard and said, "You do that, but it's going to be after I bust you up."

Then he heard a voice from behind him. "Gentlemen, would you restrain yourselves?" Yak stood, and Eason started to speak, but Walsh interrupted. "I was right over there, Breezy, and I heard and saw everything."

"Then you'll run this bum off?"

"That time may come, but it hasn't just yet. Yak is right. I've watched how he goes behind you to fix the problems you create. It's true that I told you we'd shoot the scene your way, but I was waiting for him to get here, so I could bounce it off him, before we

180

actually do it. Now, General Custer may have been a fool to let himself get trapped like he did, but we need to make Errol Flynn look like a hero, and I won't have this picture derailed by bad press. Yak worries about the people, and I worry about my film. If I let you cripple or kill someone, the papers will crucify me. And, remember it was Errol who complained when your stunts killed all those horses five years ago. We've had to deal with the Humane Association on every picture since."

Eason worked his way back onto his feet. "Are you firing me?"

"Nobody's getting fired. You have good ideas, Breezy, and you do a great job with action, but nothing is done without Yak's approval. Now, you can keep that between the three of us. I'm not trying to embarrass you, but that's the way it will be." With that, Walsh gave a simple nod and left.

"I'm sorry it had to go this way, Breezy."

"Sorry? You don't know what sorry is, till you see this movie fall on its butt, because you and Walsh wouldn't let me do my job."

* * *

Audrea answered the doorbell to find a short, round man holding a fedora. "Good morning, Mr. Spawn. Is there something I can do for you?"

"We need to talk about your boys."

"Well, won't you come in?"

"I can say everything I need to say right here. Now, you know they've been doing some chores for me, and I told them they could ride my horses, when they finished. I thought it was a little funny when they'd bring the horses home all sweaty, but they brushed them down, and I didn't worry too much about it. But it made me curious, so I let them leave yesterday and then followed them. Well, sir, there they were riding a breakneck speed, jumping off, and falling down hills."

"Oh my."

"So, I went up to them and said, 'What in the world are you doing?' And, they tell me they're practicing stunts. Now, I don't mind them riding and all, but they can't be doing that kind of stuff. Anyhow, I told them they can't ride anymore. I'll still pay them for their chores, but they've got to stay off them horses."

"I'm so sorry, Mr. Spawn, and thank you for telling me. We'll take care of this as soon as their father gets home. You won't have any more trouble from those two."

* * *

The day had run long, Yak had performed six stunts, and he was dead tired. Audrea greeted him with a kiss on the cheek and said, "You look worn out. Why don't you grab a bath, and I'll get dinner on the table?"

"Oh, that sounds great. Anything happen today?"

"Just the usual. I'll tell you all about it tonight."

There was something in her tone of voice that left him unsettled. Had he forgotten something? It's not her birthday, is it? No, that's next month. He spoke to the boys, as he entered the bathroom, and then he dropped his dusty clothes. The warm water welcomed him and eased his sore muscles. And, he thought about how blessed he was to have a nice home, a wife who loves him, and three healthy children. Life was good. He stepped out of the tub and dried himself, as water gurgled down the drain. In a few moments, he was dressed and taking his seat at the dinner table. Audrea filled his glass with water, and he asked, "What's up with you boys today?"

"Nothing, Daddy," they both chimed.

"Do you mean you spent all day out there, and nothing happened? I guess you boys lead dull lives." He scooped some mashed potatoes onto his plate. "What is that, pot roast?"

"Yes, I made it special for tonight, because Tap and Joe like it so much. Don't you, boys?" They nodded without speaking.

Yak bit into a slice of meat, looked around the table, and said, "Something ain't right here. Have you boys been up to something?" Again, they shook their heads. "Audrea?"

"Oh, are you asking me about my day?"

"Well, yeah."

"Let's see. I went down to the schoolhouse, and Tap's teacher told me a very interesting story about him. It seems he and his friends were acting out in class. She got so frustrated that she told him he could go jump out the window."

"You're not going to tell me he actually did, are you?"

"Two stories high. Scared the poor woman nearly to death. And, if that's not enough, Mr. Spawn come over. He's been kind enough to let our boys ride his horses, and what do they do? They ride them up and down a hilltop, jumping off like a bunch of wild Indians. Do you know what he said, Yak? I'll tell you. He says Tap and Joe can't ride those horses anymore, because they're wearing them out, and he doesn't want our children breaking their necks on his property. Now, what I want to know, Mr. Canutt, is what are you going to do with your children?"

Yak crossed his legs and said, "Well, first I'm going to finish my dinner. Then I'm going to smoke my pipe, and when I'm through with that, maybe around nine o'clock, I'm going wear their butts out. Would that suit you, Mrs. Canutt?"

She smiled and ran her sardonic, mother's gaze across her two sons. "Eat your supper, boys. I made pie."

* * *

"Where are we going, Daddy?" Tap asked, as his father drove the family car out of North Beverly Hills onto the movie lot in Culver City.

"You don't need to worry about that. I'm still pretty mad at you two boys. It looks like I can't trust you enough to leave you at home. You're about to worry your mother to death, jumping off the house, riding the neighbor's horses till they nearly drop. Do you think I want to take you to work with me? No, sir. I've got work to do, and I don't know how I'm going to do it with two rabble rousers like you around. And, I'll tell you this. You'd better listen to everything I tell you today. A movie set is no place to be fooling around." He glanced over the seat back. "And, that goes for you too, Joe."

"We'll be good. I promise."

"You'd better be. My gosh, Tap, you're old enough to drive. How am I supposed to trust you on the road, if you can't listen to what we tell you?"

"Okay, okay. You don't have to make such a big deal of it."

Yak parked near a jungle scene on the backlot. He marched his sons to a pair of chairs behind the camera and said, "Now, you stay here and watch. I've got to work with an animal trainer on a stunt with his bear."

"Do bears live in the jungle?" Joe asked.

"They do in this movie." His boys were a handful, almost as wild as he was as their ages. He pointed a finger at them and walked to an elderly man standing next to a steel cage. "Good morning, Mr. Haliat. I'm Yakima Canutt, and I'll be directing the stunt with your bear today."

"Himmie. His name is Himmie."

"Yes, sir, I'll try to remember that. Now, I'm going to step over there and, when I get there, would you please bring Himmie out of his cage? We need to get him in front of that big bush, and then we'll shoot him standing on his hind legs growling. Do you think you can get him to do that?"

"Of course, I can, but why is that man holding a rifle?"

"It's just a precaution. We did a scene yesterday with a lion, a beautiful animal. He was supposed to cross an opening and, once off camera, he would go into a cage. Well, it turned out he was more interested in the guy on top of the cage than he was in going in it. It was a scary couple of minutes. I should know. I was the guy."

"Oh, you don't need to worry about Himmie. He would never hurt anyone."

"Well, I guess we're all set then." As he walked past the cameras, he picked a piece of rope off the ground. "What's that doing out here?" He sat next to Joe, working the rope between his hands and watching Haliat coax his big pet out of the cage.

The old man eased the bear to the bush, leaned close, and said, "Give Daddy a kiss." Without so much as a growl, Himmie bit off the end of his nose and slapped him down. Haliat disappeared under the bear's wide body, as it mauled him, and he yelled, "Don't kill Himmie. Don't kill Himmie."

Yak bounded out of his chair, leaped onto Himmie's back, and looped the piece of rope around his neck. He pulled with all his might, but the bear was too strong. It reared up and threw him off. "Don't shoot it, not yet!" Himmie stood on his hind legs and bellowed a growl that shook the set. Yak turned to the cameraman. "Are you getting that." He nodded, and Yak looked back at the bear. Its gaze ran from him to Haliat and back. "Oh, boy, this is not going to be good." He started to yell for his boys to run, but the old man staggered to his feet, blood spurting from his nose and face, and he called, "Himmie, come on. Go back inside." The drool dripping from his teeth told Yak that Himmie was going nowhere, but to his surprise, he dropped to all fours and trotted into his cage.

Yak pointed to one of the crewmen. "Get Mr. Haliat to the medic." He plopped back down in his chair and said, "That's the kind of thing that can happen in stunts, boys. Did you learn anything from it?"

Tap turned a wide grin and said, "Yeah. Never try to kiss a bear."

* * *

The war finally ended with Yakima's contribution limited to movies like *Remember Pearl Harbor* and *The Fighting Seabees.* He teamed with Rocky Lane again for Night Train to Memphis and doubled for Roy Rogers in half-a-dozen westerns. All the while he was growing older and, and at long last, he won his chance to direct.

Yak pulled a black stallion to a halt and stepped down. "That's some horse, Rocky. Thanks for letting me ride him."

"Anytime." Allan Lane took the reins and said, "Yeah, Black Jack is something else. I think he might be a bigger star than I am."

"Don't let that happen. They did it to me with Rex. He got top billing."

"How'd you feel about that?"

"Oh, not so bad. I'm directing my second movie, and he's probably in some glue bottle by now."

"Well, for my money, you should've been directing a long time ago. I think the studios saw what you could do with action and took advantage, but that's the movie business."

"I hear you're getting married soon."

"Yes, I am. Her name is Sheila Ryan, and she's a swell kid."

"It can be a good life, if you get the right one. That's my wife over by that tree. She wanted to see us shoot a scene, so I brought her along today. Well, are you guys ready to wrap this thing up?" Lane nodded, and Yak walked off camera and stood next to Audrea.

"What are they going to do?" she asked.

"This is the very end of the movie. Rocky has knocked the villain off and stopped the stagecoach. He tells Nugget . . ."

"That's the funny guy, right?"

"Comic relief. You can't make one of these westerns without someone to play the clown. Anyway, when Rocky tells him the girl is the one named Leslie, not him, Nugget faints." He raised a hand and said, "All right, let's do it. Action!" He watched the scene unfold and, as Rocky reveals the girl's identity, Nugget falls backwards. "No, no, that's not it, Eddy. You faint and fall forward, toward the camera."

Waller righted himself and said, "I think it goes better if I fall against the stage."

Yak walked around the camera. "If you do that, we lose your facial expression. The people won't see that goofy look."

"Goofy? Hey, I've played this kind of role in a lot of movies, and I have never been called goofy."

"I'm not calling you goofy, and maybe I could've used a better word. We want to get that classic, comic face, the one you do so well. Okay? We got your version. Now, let's give my way a chance, and we'll pick the better one later. Will you do that?"

"Well, it's your movie, I guess, but my way is better. I know what I'm talking about."

The film was almost over, and Yak was doing his best to keep from having one of his stars walk off the lot. He lit a cigarette on his way back to Audrea and muttered, "That man drives me crazy."

"Really? That funny, little guy?"

"His character is funny. He ain't. I thought my problems would be with Mildred Coles. She's a classically trained, dramatic actress, but she's been great. But Eddy has been a problem from the first day. His own special coffee every morning, bananas for snacks, lemon drops. Can you believe that? We're in Bronson Canyon for heaven's sake. How am I supposed to keep him supplied with his little treats?" He threw down his smoke. "I even agreed to have my name shown last in the opening credits. What else can I do to satisfy these people?" Yak collected himself, and called for action again.

* * *

The day ended, and Yakima Canutt, the director, had his movie in the can. He said little until they reached the main road, and then he let it out. "I'm sorry, baby, but this directing thing just ain't working."

"Are you sure? I mean, you've only done two movies. I thought the first one was great, and I'm sure this one will be."

"It's a good movie. Rocky will do well with it. I just don't have the patience for the phonies. Aw, I don't mean that. Eddy's not a bad guy, but he grates on my nerves, and I probably do the same to him."

"But directing has been your dream."

"And, it still is, but I'm better suited to direct actions scenes, not the whole movie. If this film taught me anything, it was that."

* * *

Dinner was over, and Yak sat smoking his pipe while John Wayne lit a cigarette. "That was real good,

190

Audrea," Wayne said. "Thanks for letting me come over.

"You know you're always welcome here." She gathered a few dishes and vanished into the kitchen.

Wayne crushed his smoke in an ash tray and said, "The reason I wanted to come, Yak, is because you might get called to testify before the House Committee on Unamerican Activities soon."

"Why would they want to talk to me. I'm no Communist."

"Nobody knows that better than I do, but they're looking for people who can name actors and producers who are."

"I read about that. They indicted a bunch of people. What did they call it? Yeah, the Hollywood Ten. Is this the same committee that was looking for Nazis back in the 30's?"

"Yes, but the focus is on reds now, and it's gotten bad. They're looking into people like Charlie Chaplin and Orson Welles. I always wondered about those guys."

"Come on, John. Just because somebody accuses you of something, that doesn't mean you're guilty. I don't think I ever met either of them, but I'm not assuming they're Communists without some proof."

"The committee is getting the proof, and part of that is talking to people like you and me."

"Did they talk to you?"

"Just informally, so far, but I don't mind whatever they want to ask me. I'm American, through and through. I'm just here to tell you to be careful."

Yak tamped his tobacco and relit it. "I'm not following you. What do I need to be careful about?"

"Friends you make. Movies you do. Did you know they interviewed John Huston?"

"Huston? They interviewed John Huston? What did he say?"

"Ah, you know how he is. He basically told them to cram it. And, later he felt bad about that, because he learned the Hollywood Ten lied to Congress. Even then, he wouldn't name names. I hope he knows what he's doing. I've known that guy for a long time, and he doesn't need to play around with the committee. They've got the FBI checking on people."

"Now, that's going a little too far. I mean, I'm for America, you know, but people have the right to believe what they want. I don't agree with that Communist stuff, but . . ."

"Be careful how loud you say that. I'm your friend, Yak, but not everyone is. Look, the other thing I came for is to tell you about a movie we're going to shoot. I want you to think about being part of it, somehow. James Arness and I play two investigators for the committee. We go to Hawaii to break up a Communist ring down there. This is the kind of movie that lets people know where you stand."

"I know where I stand, with my wife and kids, and I don't want my children to grow up in a country where the government has to approve who their friends are."

"Nobody's saying that. We just want to get the bad guys out of our business, before they wreck it. If they call you, the first question will be, 'Are you now or have you ever been a member of the Communist Party?' And, the second question will be about whether you know anyone who is."

"If we have people spying for Russia, then let's find them and execute them. I'll even serve on the firing squad. Otherwise, I don't rat on my friends, John, and I don't condemn people based on rumors. Now, the truth is that I don't know who's a Communist and who ain't."

"That's good enough. You say that and you've got nothing to worry about."

"I'm beginning to think I have a lot to worry about. We all do."

* * *

A long day at the backlot left him weary. Yakima stopped his car next to the porch, glanced at the '32 Chevy parked in his drive, and found Audrea waiting for him at the door. "Hey, baby. Did somebody's car break down in our driveway?"

"No, that little prize belongs to Tap."

"Where did he get the money to buy some piece of junk like that? And, why did he cut off the doors and hood?"

"You know he's been working at Mr. Flower's welding shop on weekends, and he said he saved the money from that, but that's not entirely true."

"What do you mean?"

"Why don't I let him tell you?" She called to her son. "Tap, come here."

A young voice sounded from the back of the house. "I'm busy."

"I don't care if you're busy. Your father is home. You get yourself in here and do it now."

Tap shuffled into the room with an adjustable wrench in his hand and his brother close behind. "Hey, Daddy. How was your day?"

Yak's sons never asked him about his day, and he sensed something was wrong. "Long, son, long. Now, tell me about that car. How did you earn the money to buy it?"

"Working down at Flower's shop."

"Is that all?"

Tap looked at his mother and then at the floor. "Well, not exactly. I sold some autographed pictures of Uncle John."

"You didn't tell people he's actually your uncle, did you?"

"Oh, no, I'd never do that. They just wanted his picture, so I sold them. You know, American ingenuity."

"Son, you know how busy he is. How could you impose on him to sign all those pictures?"

Then Audrea stepped in. "He didn't. Tell him what you did, Tap."

"I, uh, snapped a picture of Uncle John the last time he was here and I took it down to the drug store to have copies made. They cost me ten cents each, and I sold them for a dollar. It was a good deal. And, like you said, I didn't want to impose on him, so I sort of signed his name."

"You sort of signed his name? That means you lied to everybody you sold one to."

"I didn't lie. I just didn't tell them all the truth."

"You're going to pay those people back, every penny. I don't care if you have to work every weekend for the rest of the year. My gosh, son, you're nearly eighteen years old. I thought we taught you better than this."

"I don't know if I can make that much money. I guess I could join the Army when school is out."

"Not with all that business going on in Korea you won't. I still don't understand what we're doing over there, but my son's not going to get his head blown off for some cause I can't explain. No, sir, if they want one of my boys, they can draft him."

"Well, can I keep the car? Joe and I are making it into a hotrod."

"You can keep it, but you can't drive it on the road.

"How am I supposed to do that, Daddy?"

"We've got more than an acre of land, the backyard opens to the desert, and the Hollywood Hills are not far. All of that is open ground. I don't think you could wreck that car out there if you tried. And, don't let your brother drive. He's not old enough." Tap lowered his gaze, and Yak stood. "Do as I say, Tap. And, don't go acting crazy out there."

* * *

With his work completed for the week, Yak slept in the next morning, ate a late breakfast, and settled into his favorite chair with the newspaper. "Would you look at that?"

Audrea poured a glass of juice for Honey and said, "Look at what?"

"This article says William Boyd is buying the rights to all his old Hopalong Cassidy movies. He's spending almost every cent he's got."

"What's he going to do with all those old movies?"

"It says he's going to cut them down to half hour shows and put them on television. I wonder if John has thought about buying up his old movies. You know, television could be as big as radio one day."

"Well, I don't guess we need to worry about buying up a bunch of movies."

"No, I couldn't raise that kind of money."

"I didn't mean to say you couldn't do it. It's just that we have a family and all."

"Speaking of family, where are those boys?"

"Out driving that car. They left early."

He folded the paper and set it aside. "Yeah, well, I think I'll go have a look." He started his truck and followed their tire tracks past scrub brush and scattered trees until he reached the back of the Hollywood sign with Los Angeles sprawling below. But he didn't come for the scenery. He needed to find his boys. Where could they be hiding? He became more worried than frustrated, and he pulled to a stop at the bottom of a steep hill. "I can't believe they drove that old heap up there. He shifted into low gear, when he heard the roar of an engine. He saw the stripped-down Chevy flash across the crest of the hill and sail off the edge of the cliff, tumbling and flipping down the steep embankment. "Oh, dear God." The tail of his pickup swerved, kicking up dirt and rocks, as he pushed it faster and faster toward the wreckage, "Sweet Jesus, don't let him be dead." He searched the battered car and found nothing. Then his gaze ran up the hill, to the top, where Tap and Joe stood laughing. Yak caught his breath for a moment, let his heart calm below panic, and then he yelled to them. "Get down here."

The laughter was gone by the time they reached their father, and Joe said, "I didn't do it."

"Tap, what in the name of all that's holy were you thinking?"

"I jumped out in time. I always do."

"Always do? You mean you've done this before?"

"Lots of times. There are three more cars on the other side of the hill. I wreck them, fix them up, and wreck them again. It's no big deal."

Yak wanted to scream at him, but Tap had the same reckless spirit he'd had when he was younger. He longed for excitement. The question now was how Yak could harness that craving. "Okay, son, I give up. I'm leaving for New Mexico tomorrow, and you're coming with me. I'll talk to the director and get him to hire you as an extra. Maybe once we get there, and you show me you can behave, then we'll let you do a few stunts."

"Really? I'm going to be a stuntman? Wait till I tell my friends. They'll go bonkers."

Then his other son spoke up. "Me too. I want to be a stuntman."

"Just hold your horses, Joe. We'll talk about you when the time comes. Now, Tap, I'm trusting you not to do anything stupid. This is a serious business, son. Don't go acting like a fool or you'll get hurt, and your mother will never forgive me."

* * *

The oppressive heat of Gallup, New Mexico burned even hotter in the middle of August. Yak and Tap walked onto the set shoulder to shoulder, and they found the director sitting on the steps of his trailer. "Gordon, I'd like for you to meet my son, Tap. Tap, this is Mr. Douglas."

Douglas stood and shook his hand. "Good morning to both of you. It's quite a steamer, huh?"

"Yes, sir. My dad told me to expect this."

"And, he told you right. Well, let me look you over. You're not as broad as your dad, but you're just as tall. Do you have his guts?"

"He's got plenty of that, maybe too much. I called ahead to see if you have a spot for him as an extra."

"Do you mean he's not following in his father's footsteps?"

"Yes, sir, I am. I want to be a stuntman, and I think I'd be good at it."

"Is that what you want, Yak?"

"I don't reckon I can stop him. He comes of age in a couple of weeks, and then it won't matter what I want. I just want to make sure he does it right."

Douglas set his clipboard down and reached up to lay his hand on Tap's shoulder. "Your father has done great things for the movie industry, and I don't mean just the fantastic stunts he's done. He made changes that save lives. I remember the days when men walked in off the streets, desperate for work, and they'd do anything. Risk their very lives for a day's wages. I used to lay awake nights, worrying about how many men would be crippled the next day, or maybe killed. But Yakima Canutt changed all that. He came up with safety devices no one had even thought about before. You couldn't have a better tutor, son."

"Thank you, Mr. Douglas. I'll do my best."

"I know you will. Now, Yak, I did get word that you'd like to have Tap work as an extra, but how do I hire the son of the greatest stuntman who ever lived and not put him in some stunts? I wouldn't be much of a director, if I did that."

"He's a good horseman, and he certainly knows how to take a fall. I've seen that firsthand. Maybe we could make him one of the Indians that attack the fort. He could get shot and do a back flip off the horse."

"I was thinking of something else. The main characters of this film are played by Gregory Peck and Michael Ansara. They're both tall and, as you know, we don't have a lot of tall stuntmen. We found someone to double Michael, but I'm not happy with my choices for Greg. Now, you've read the script, Yak. If we give Tap a chance at doubling the star, we're going to need consistency in appearance. He has to do all the stunts, not just tackling people off horses and fights. That includes that scene near the end of the movie."

"He can do it, but if you're worried about that, why not shoot that scene first?"

Douglas grinned and said, "I thought of that too. It's an easy setup, just Tap and the camera crew. We should be ready in an hour. Take him over to wardrobe and make sure he understands what we expect." He turned back to Tap. "If it's too much for you, son, just say so. There's no shame in it."

As Douglas walked away, Tap asked, "What is that supposed to mean?"

"It's a wide shot of the Army captain running away from a mountain pass just before it blows to bits. You've got to be close enough for the audience to believe you're in real danger. You'll have to cinch your pants up tight for that one."

* * *

Yak stood next to the one camera assigned to shoot the scene. "Can you hold on a minute? I need to make sure about something." The cameraman nodded, and Yak sprinted across the dusty ground to a pair of boulders where Tap stood, wiping the sweat from his face. "Are you all right, son?"

"Fine, just a little hot. That's all."

"You run right toward that camera, and keep your head down, so it doesn't pick up your face."

"I know, I know. You told me a dozen times."

"It's going to be really loud, but I set the charges myself, so I know they're okay. We seldom really blow anything up in Hollywood. We want noise and dust, so much it looks like Judgement Day, but it ain't. We do need enough dynamite and fullers earth to make it look real, but don't let it spook you."

"Daddy, are we going to have this conversation every time I do a stunt?"

"No, I'm just trying to, well, okay. It's your job. I guess I need to let you do it. Good luck, son." He jogged back to the camera, held up one hand, and then yelled, "Action!" Tap stood still for a moment, then he ran between two boulders, turned, and drew his pistol. The explosion was enormous, shaking the very ground where Yak stood, and he whispered, "Dear God, let him be safe." As much as he wanted to run to his boy, he didn't. It was time for Tap to be a man, and time for Yak to let him be one. The scene ended, and another Canutt was in the stunt business.

Chapter Nine

The beauty of Africa rose to Yakima's eyes, as his plane soared over the Congo River and then across the Gulf of Guinea to French Equatorial Africa. He could hardly take it all in, vast jungles spreading for miles on end, and an occasional mountain peak jutting from the trees. This was a long way from the Snake River, and his studio had warned him that the customs would be just a strange as the scenery. He landed at Brazzaville and booked a room at the Rellias De Maya Hotel. He unpacked, showered, and changed clothes before going down to the restaurant for dinner and to meet the man he brought in from France. And, he greeted him with a handshake. "You must be Gilles."

"Oui, oh, pardon me. Yes, I am Gilles Bonneau." He was a rugged-looking man, firm of body, with a chiseled, tanned face. "I took the liberty of ordering two glasses of wine. I hope you like Cabernet. Shall we get down to business?"

"I'm afraid I like wine a little too much, but I'll have one glass with you. When I started on this project, they told me the two best men in the world with gorillas were you and Bill Said. Since Bill died in a car wreck last year, that left you. So, I asked our contacts in London to make a deal. I wasn't sure about hiring someone I've never met, but by the look of you, I think you'll do."

"I have been here for a few days and talked to the local authorities. If you have never been to Africa, you may find things very different here. The wheels of government move slowly unless one greases them with a few commissions. Do you understand?"

"Money. It's the universal language. They kept my guns at customs. Can you get them out?"

"I cannot, but Monsieur Blancou can. He is the head of the game department, and we are friends. Oh, and, you will need a hunting license."

"I don't want the guns to hunt. I just want them to protect us, if the gorillas go crazy. Why would, oh, commissions, right?" Bonneau smiled without answering. "Okay, I have money, but don't let them bleed me dry." The waiter arrived with two glasses and a bottle of wine. He said something in French, and Yak tapped his finger on the table. "Would you ask him if they have a steak and maybe some potatoes?"

"Of course." They exchanged a few more words he didn't understand, Bonneau brushed the waiter away, and said, "You will have your steak. I cannot promise what kind of animal it will come from, but it will be steak."

"That sounds good. Now, I want to get started as soon as we can. We'll be shooting process plates, the background the director will use with the principal actors. I need lots of gorillas and, most importantly, I need to film a big gorilla charging at the camera. I can't go back without that shot."

"Ah, you want the Garcon, the Big Boy. It will not be easy to get an animal to behave the way you wish for him to behave in the wild. It is their home, not ours."

"I don't plan to film it in the wild. There wouldn't be enough light for the cameras. We'll build a kind of jungle arena about the size of a football field. American football. We'll surround it with fences, sort of like a big corral. If they can help us find a savannah near the edge of the jungle, that would work great. We locate a family of gorillas and drive them into it. Once we have control of them, we'll get our shots and then let them go."

"Yes, perhaps that could work. I spoke with Monsieur Blancou, and he told me the forest of Gabon, north of Ewo, has recently been opened for hunting gorillas."

"We're going to need a lot of locals to help drive the gorillas to the arena, probably five or six hundred. I've been reading a lot of books on Africa, and they all say the tribes do whatever their chief and witch doctor tell them to do. How do we go about getting the people we need?"

"You have hit on the problem precisely. In order to get the cooperation of tribesmen, you must win over the chief. Then we must bring the witch doctor on board, so he does not put a curse on us."

"Geez, this sounds like dealing with the Nez Perce medicine men. If you can set that up for next week, I'll get with Johnny Pallet to find a location and start work on a base camp."

"Very well, but don't be too optimistic. These people are not your Nez Perce. If they think you are here to harm them, they will cut your throat, and mine with you."

* * *

After three weeks of hard work, the base camp was complete, with a kitchen, dining room and two barracks. Now came the time to recruit hunters to help locate and drive a family of gorillas. Yakima sat in the passenger's seat of a Dodge power wagon, as Bonneau drove them deep into the jungle. "Why do we have to meet with them in the middle of the night? This would be a lot simpler during the daylight."

"It would be simpler for us, Monsieur Yak, but these tribes need a certain pageantry. They look more ominous and foreboding in the flicker of firelight."

"No, I get it. If they want to keep the people under their fingers, they need to keep them superstitious, and that calls for mystery. It reminds me of those snake-handling preachers, who used to come through Seattle back in the Twenties."

"And, we must respect those superstitions, if we are to get their help. I should tell you, there is a danger. If we offend the chief, they could kill us."

206

Yak patted his jacket and said, "They'd better have a bunch of them, if they want to do that. Because the first six won't see morning."

"Let's hope it doesn't come to that. By the way, what is in those two bags in the back of the truck?"

"You'll see when we get there. This is my first time in Africa, but it ain't my first time negotiating a deal." By the time they reached the village of Okalataka, the tribe members were already seated around a large fire chanting. "Who's the skinny, little guy next to the chief?" Yak asked.

"He is the interpreter. I hired him in Ewo. He speaks French and their dialect. He will translate to me, and I will translate to you. The interpreter has already told them why we are here, so we can get right to work on the negotiations." A man across the circle made some clicking noises and then began to rattle off something and shake his fist. "He says gorillas cannot be herded, and you are crazy to try capturing them just to take their pictures."

"Well, at least they know what a picture is. I wasn't sure about that."

"Yes, Europeans have been in this part of Africa for centuries. These people continue to live this way because they choose to."

"Tell him we may be crazy, but we'll pay them well for their work."

"I will tell the chief that we will pay him well. The others will do as he says." A few words were exchanged, and Bonneau said, "He wants to see our money."

"Time to ante up, huh?" Yak drew a circle in the dirt. He reached into his pocket, took out the money he'd agreed to pay, and laid it in the circle. "There, every nickel we told them we'd pay." A stir arose around the fire, men chattering in ways Yak could not understand. "What's all that about?"

"The men are telling their stories about gorillas. One says a Garcon bit off part of his hand, because he was trespassing on the gorilla's territory."

"How would he know why the gorilla bit him?"

"Because the gorilla told him."

"Oh, that's a lot of . . ."

"Don't scoff too quickly, my friend. These people believe the gorillas are people. When someone says a gorilla spoke to them, they believe it is true. They trust the gorilla, but they do not trust us."

"Let me see if I can fix that." He walked to the truck, opened one of his bags, and came back with two jugs of wine. When he set them in the circle, the chief passed them around. "I didn't go too far in school, but they did teach me about the common denominator, and a good bottle of hooch speaks a common language." Within half an hour, the tribesmen were singing, and they had a deal.

* * *

Yak, Bonneau, and seven hundred natives were in place before the sun rose. "It's going to be a beautiful morning," Bonneau said.

"I hope so. We covered everything with the tribesmen again last night. They'll keep moving in, firing their blanks and yelling, while the rest follow with the nets. Little by little, we work the gorillas into the open end of the arena."

"And, what if the gorillas attack them?"

"They are to fire their rifles. That should back them off. If not, we'll shoot. Nobody's going to get killed out here, not if I can help it." He took a chew of tobacco and said, "I've hunted everything from muskrats to grizzlies, but this is the strangest hunt I've ever been on."

"Muskrats?"

"Yeah, it's a scruffy, little animal, but it tastes pretty good. Anyway, I hope these critters don't sneak up behind us."

"Oh, he will not, monsieur. When the Garcon comes, you will know it."

They pressed on into the jungle, drums pounding and rifles firing. One hour, two hours, and then three. Then the men stopped, and their drums went silent. Yak didn't know the jungle, but the natives did, and he sensed they felt something in the air. He brought his rifle up, as the leaves began to rustle. A fierce, guttural sound came from the trees, vines snapped, and a massive gorilla charged at Yak. The hunters fired their rifles into the air, and the gorilla stopped. He snorted, threw dirt, and hissed. Then he leapt back into the trees and disappeared. Yak lowered his gun and said, "I thought they had a lot of bluff in them. He ain't so different from a grizzly."

"Don't underestimate the gorilla."

"I ain't. When I say he's like a grizzly, that's a compliment, but the griz can be bluffed, and so can that big boy. All right, let's get on with it. We've got to get these monkeys to their new home." Over the course of the next two hours, thirteen gorillas passed through the opening into the arena, and Yak's crew closed them in. All was set to get his footage, or at least it seemed to be.

* * *

Yak gave the gorillas two days to settle into their new habitat, and then he set up the cameras. He built cages to protect the cameramen, with openings just wide enough for their lenses. But someone had to be outside, someone to lure the Garcon toward the camera for the key shot. And, that someone would be him. He stood at a worktable, stuffing straw into a human dummy, as Bonneau approached with the witch doctor. "Monsieur Yak, we have a problem."

"Do you mean a problem with him?"

"Yes. As you see, he has a basket, and he says the basket contains a small gorilla. If he releases the gorilla, it will run away, and then the natives will kill the other gorillas."

"Why would they want to do that? It doesn't make sense."

"Nonetheless."

"Okay, okay, how much does he want?"

"Twenty francs."

"How much is that in American money?"

"Perhaps five dollars."

Yak dug into his pocket and handed over the money. He watched the witch doctor smile and walk away. "Geez, I hate dealing with politicians." He finished his dummy and tied it to the end of a long stick with a two-foot lanyard. When he entered the arena, he called to the cameramen. "Okay, guys, start shooting and keep rolling, no matter what." He called on his most inner courage and walked into the clearing, yelling, "Hey, big boy. Where are you? Come on down." He continued to call and wave the dummy until he heard the same snarling and rumble in the trees he'd heard before. As the Garcon appeared, Yak kept waving the dummy, as he backed his way toward the camera and out of its range. The gorilla stood on its hind legs and bellowed its primal screams. It was dramatic, savage, and visceral, but it wasn't enough. Yak needed more. He waved the dummy again, but the big boy didn't move. So, he threw it down, raised his arms, and took a step forward. The gorilla pounded its chest and charged. It was almost too close before Yak drew his pistol and pointed it at its head. The gorilla skidded to a stop, shook himself, and cried out. Yak cocked the hammer, but the gorilla had seen enough. He turned and bolted back into the brush.

Yak put his pistol away and drew a long, exasperated breath. "Somebody, tell me you got that." Every cameraman at every angle said yes. "Thank God. I sure don't want to do that again, not now, not ever."

When he reached the dining area, he sat down with Bonneau and a cup of coffee. "Well, Gilles, I don't mind telling you, that big, old gorilla had me going for a minute there."

"You did well, my friend. And, now you must kill it."

"Kill it? No. I told you we came here to film them, not kill them."

"It is the custom of these people. I told you before, they believe the gorillas are people, and they have made war on those people. If they let the Garcon go, he will come back to take revenge on their women and children. He must die, and you must do it."

"Not a chance. We got the footage we want and then some. We're going to pack up our stuff and go home."

"Very well, but if you don't kill the Garcon, they will, and they will kill all his family as well."

"You can't be serious about this. I mean, these people are kind of, you know, backwards, but once I got to know them, I liked them. They're basically good people."

"They have their beliefs, just like you have yours. If you told them a man was crucified and came back to life, they would laugh at you. And, we mock them for wanting to kill the Garcon. This is their life, Yak. Either you kill him or the family dies."

Yak threw his cup against the wall, picked up his rifle, and said, "One thing I learned from my Indian friends is to respect the animal you hunt, but I'm not feeling very respectful right now. Get everything loaded into the trucks. When this is done, I want to go home."

* * *

Evening was beginning to fall, when Yakima finally reached home. He paid the taxi driver, dropped his valise and two cases on the porch, and swept Audrea into his arms. He hugged her long and hard, gave her a warm kiss, and said, "I thought I'd never get home."

"I was starting to worry."

"Yeah, I got delayed in New York, something to do with a prop on the plane, but here I am. So, where are the kids?"

"Tap's working on a night shoot at the studio. And, I sent Joe and Honey to spend the night with some friends. We've got the house all to ourselves."

"That's my girl."

"Come on, dinner's on the table. Pork chops, mashed potatoes, and green peas."

"That sounds great. You wouldn't believe the things I ate in Africa." He put his things away and took his seat before a sumptuous meal. "I guess I shouldn't complain too much about the food over there. Some of

213

it was pretty good. I just didn't always know what it was."

Audrea passed him the pitcher of water and asked, "Do those cases have your film from the trip?"

"Yeah. The airline wanted me to put them in the storage compartment, but there was no way I'd let them get out of my sight. I put too much work into getting those shots to trust them to somebody else. I called the studio from New York to tell them I was on my way, and we're going to screen the film in the morning."

"Who's going to screen them with you?"

"Oh, John Ford, Clark Gable, and probably the screen writer, John Mahin. Gable wants to see everything, and that causes him and Pappy not to get along too well. Ford says Gable asks for too many retakes, and Gable thinks Ford isn't thorough enough. Once this movie is done, I'm not sure they'll ever work together again."

"That's a shame. I only met Clark Gable once, but he seemed very nice."

"He is. You know he's nearly as old as I am, but he doesn't try to hide it. He doesn't dye the gray in his hair or use a lot of makeup to cover his wrinkles. But he's a stickler when it comes to his movies. He wants every scene to be the best it can be, no matter how many times they have to shoot it."

She took his hand and said, "Well, all those women out there can have Clark Gable. I just want my man, and I want him tonight." They spent that evening like it was their first, except there was no howling dog to keep them awake this time.

* * *

Yak sat in the screening room between Gable and Ford, who had Mahin to his right with a notepad in his lap. Gable leaned over to Yak and whispered, "I hope you know how sorry I am about what happened to you in *Boomtown*."

"Those things happen. It wasn't your fault."

"Maybe not, but you nearly got killed doubling for me."

"Is that why you helped me get this job?"

"I didn't help you with this. Pappy worked with you before, and so did I. We both thought you were the man for the job, the only man for it."

As the film began to roll, Ford muttered, "Oh, I like that. I didn't know gorillas would beat their chests in the top of a tree."

"Yes, sir," Yak answered. "They were pretty upset about being caught in the arena. The locals told us they wouldn't eat in captivity, but I said any animal will eat when it gets hungry enough, and they did. You can see how healthy they look. But they were really ticked off."

Ford continued to watch, as the spectacle of nature rolled before him. "I love this stuff, Yak. Oh, wow, what was that?"

"That's the Garcon charging toward the camera."

"Yes, I can see that, but how did you get him to do it?"

"I stood beside the camera, shaking a dummy on a stick, and he didn't do much, so I threw the dummy down and started doing everything he did. When he kicked dirt, I kicked dirt. And, that got him riled up."

"You're lucky he didn't kill you. I'm glad you got the shot, but I didn't send you over there to take those kinds of chances."

"I knew he was bluffing."

Ford turned to his screenwriter. "Put that into the script, the part of about the gorilla bluffing."
Then Gable interrupted. "How close were you when he charged?"

"Too close, but I couldn't get the affect standing behind a screen. The gorilla needed to believe he could get at me."

"It's great footage. He is a mean-looking ape."

Yak looked away for a moment and then said, "The sad part is that I had to shoot him. If I hadn't, the locals were going to kill all the gorillas, and I couldn't see that happen."

"Did you get it on film?" Ford asked.

"I didn't want to, but I did. It's at the end."

"Okay, we can work that into the movie."

Gable crossed his legs and lit a cigarette. "You know, John, it's becoming more clear to me that you guys are doing your best to make an actor like me look like the man Yakima Canutt really is. Maybe he should be the star of this movie."

Ford stood without answering. "Okay, let's get this stuff over to the cutting room, and I'll start picking out the parts I want. Why don't you take the afternoon off, Yak? Go spend some time with that wife of your."

"Thanks, John, but I already took care of that."

* * *

Honey Canutt's seventeenth birthday brought her to a department store in Culver City to buy a new outfit with her mother. She ran her hand down the rack of clothes and said, "Why do we always shop in the bargain aisle? It's so embarrassing. What if somebody sees me?"
"Let them see you. We're not rich people, and we don't pretend to be."

"We're kind of rich. Daddy works in the movie business. We have a big house."

"Yes, your daddy has done well for us, but it wasn't always that way. The first few years we were married were a struggle. Your father was lucky to get any work with so many unemployed during the Depression. And, my job at the telephone company sure didn't pay enough to cover the bills. We know what it's like to do without, and you're not going to waste what we have now." She held out a blue-and-white, striped dress. "Why don't you try this one on? It's your size."

"Oh, Mama. Girls don't wear that anymore. I want a pant suit."

"Young girls don't wear pants in this family. I'll buy pants for your brothers and your daddy, but not for you. You're going to be a lady, if it kills me."

"Lady, schmady. If Daddy was here, he'd let me wear pants."

"Well, he's not here and he won't be home for probably two years. When he gets back, then you can ask him for some pants."

"I wish he was home now. What's he doing over there, anyway?"

"Something to do with horses. He had to buy and train a bunch of horses, and now he's working on some kind of racetrack for that new movie."

"The one with Charlton Heston?" Audrea nodded. "Oh, I think he's just dreamy. Is Daddy going to meet him?"

"I'm sure he will. Once they get all the horses trained, your father has to teach him and another actor how to drive a chariot. That's all I know right now. It takes a long time for letters to travel from Italy to California, and telephone calls are really expensive. We're going to have to be patient until he gets home. And, until he does, I'm the head of this household, and that means you don't wear pants."

"I was home when the mailman came today. You got a letter from Aunt Sally. Is she coming to visit?"

"Well, you are little Miss Nosey, aren't you? I wasn't going to tell you until later, but your father sent me an airline ticket, so I can watch them film the race scene. Your Aunt Sally is going to watch you while I'm gone."

"I don't need anybody to watch me. I'm a grown woman."

"Not yet, you aren't, and I'm not going to be on the other side of the ocean without somebody here to keep an eye on you. I've seen how you look at that Dittman boy."

"Tommy's nice. Besides, Daddy knows him. He's a stuntman too."

"Man is the word I'm talking about. He's too old for you."

"No, he's not. You weren't much older than me when you married Daddy."

"I know how old I was, and I know how old you are. And, let me tell you, girl, you are not ready for that. So, you have a choice. You can stay with your Aunt Sally, or I can put you in a convent till I get back. What's it going to be?"

"I love Aunt Sally."

* * *

"I know they're Lipizzaner stallions, but tell him I won't pay that much." Yak waited impatiently, as the interpreter conveyed his message to the horses' owner in Italian.

"He says he must have his price."

"Okay, tell him this. I only need the horses long enough to make the movie. Once it's over, he can have them back. We're talking rent here. I've already got seventy horses. I can get by without his."

A shake of the owner's head sent Yak walking away, until he heard a voice say, "All right, you have a deal."

He turned back to the man. "So, you spoke English the whole time. Okay, bring them over to the corral, and we'll get you the money." The man led the horses away, and Yak looked at the interpreter. "Those are Arabians. I would've paid him a lot more than what he was asking, but I won't be lied to. He understood every word I said. I could see that from the beginning."

He now had a full complement of blacks and whites for the two principal chariots. Yak drove back to the set outside Rome. The movie's Colosseum was nearing completion, but his interest lay in the practice track outside. It was the same dimensions as the real track, but without stands around it. He knelt by one of the chariots and mumbled, "I told them I wanted gooseneck tongues."

"What's the matter, Yak? Are you down there, praying?"

Yak stood and shook Heston's hand. "I'll tell you, Chuck, we could use a little prayer for this picture."

"You've been teaching me how to drive this chariot for nearly a week on this practice track. When do we go into the Colosseum and try it?"

"Not today, but I'm going in there in a little while. I tried to tell them not to build the track the way they did, but Henry Henixson won't listen, and he's got Mr. Zimbalist snowed."

"What's wrong with the track?"

"They're worried about rain, so they dug up the top soil and put in a layer of rock for drainage. Then they covered it back up with sand and threw in some cement dust. The sand is too soft for the chariot wheels. It's going to wear the horses out, and any moisture in that sand will make a layer of concrete. None of that is good for the race."

"Do I need to go talk to them?"

"No, don't do that. We're supposed to try it out with half a dozen chariots later today. If I'm right, it will show. And, if I'm wrong, they probably won't listen to me again. Now, let's get to work." Heston stepped onto the chariot with Yak standing behind him. "Okay, just like we did before. Take them around slowly a couple of times, and then give them their heads. Lean the way I showed you, and the chariot will slide around the turn. If it feels like too much, just hand me the reins."

"I have to admit I'm still a little nervous."

"Don't' be. Just drive the chariot, and I guarantee you'll win the race."

"They tell me your son, Joe, is going to double for me. Is that right?"

"Yes. He's twenty-one now, and he's been stunting for several years. Besides, he learned to drive wagons at my mother's ranch when he was ten, and has driven stagecoaches in a couple of movies. He should do fine with this. He won't embarrass you."

"I didn't think he would."

Heston brought the team to a trot and circled the track. "Okay, Chuck, let's bring them up to a gallop." Another circuit, and Yak said, "Here you go. Open them up." As Heston snapped the reins, Yak stepped off. He watched him skid around the first turn, dash up the far straightaway, and skid again around the second turn. Heston pulled to a stop beside Yak and said, "That was a dirty trick."

"Yeah, it was, but you did great."

He grinned, scratched his head, and answered. "Yes, I did, didn't I? You know, I'm beginning to think we might actually pull this off."

Chapter Ten

The day was growing late when Yak reached the set.
He stood next to the enormous obelisk that watched
over the first turn, and said nothing. The six drivers
brought their chariots to the starting line, and
Zimbalist called out, "Give me a good run, gentlemen.
Now, go." Two chariots sunk so deep into the sand
they never got off the line. One flipped going around
the turn, and the other three ran afoul on the
backstretch. Zimbalist and Henixson ran to the driver
who had wrecked and helped him to his feet. Yak
walked down to the track and said, "This track is
impossible. The chariots sink in the sand, and the
horses can't get up any speed in it. They're practically
dehydrated from trying. And, when they reach the
turns, they slide on that layer of concrete."

Henixson adjusted his black-rimmed glasses.
"There's nothing wrong with this track. I talked to
every one of your drivers, and they told me it was
fine."

Yak called for the driver who had fallen. "Jerry, did
you tell Mr. Henixson this track was okay to work on?"

"Absolutely not. I told him it was no good to work
on, and I'll say it again. This track is lousy."

"All right, Henixson. Tell me the names of the drivers who told you this track is okay."

Henixson scoffed at him. "You say the horses slid on concrete. I could stick my thumb through it."

Yak knelt beside them, and scraped the dirt away. Then he stood and said, "Do you see that? It's concrete. Go ahead. Let me see you poke your thumb through this." Henixson didn't move. "Hey, Jerry, get Mr. Henixson a pick, will you?"

Zimbalist laid his hand on Henixson's shoulder. "There's no arguing with this, Henry. Yak is going to build this track the way he wants it, and you're going to give him all the help he needs. Are we clear on that?"

Yak offered his hand, but Henixson refused it. "If that's how you want it, fine. Just do your job this time."

* * *

"Good morning everybody. Sorry to be late, but I had to pick up my wife and daughter. I hope you don't mind if they sit in on the screening."

Sol Seigel turned in his chair and said, "Not at all, Yak. Show your ladies where to sit, and we'll get started. Now, I want everyone to pay close attention. This is the chariot race from the original *Ben Hur*. It's a great scene, but we've got to do better. So, keep that in mind as we watch."

As the lights went down, Honey whispered to her father, "Thanks for sending me a ticket, Daddy."

"That's all right, baby girl. I'm glad you're here." She watched for a few minutes and asked, "Why don't they turn up the sound?"

"There's not any sound. It's a silent movie from 1925."

"Oh, how square." When the film clip ended, and the lights came back up, she said, "Geez, that was pretty good. The bad guy had those crazy eyes."

"That's Messala. Stephen Boyd is going to play that part this time. He's a terrific actor. If we get the chance, I'll introduce you."

Seigel edged his way down an aisle between the chairs, shook hands with Audrea and Honey, then said, "Did you get any new ideas, Yak?"

"One or two. In the scenes where Messala is trying to wreck the other chariots, we could add big spikes to the hub of his wheels. When he pulls his horses into theirs, the spikes tear up the other driver's wheels."

"But that doesn't seem fair."

"Well, we're talking about the villain, and this is supposed to be ancient Rome. They fed people to lions just for the sport of it. I don't think they were worried about being fair."

"You make a good point. Can you do it without hurting anyone?"

"Sure. We'll make two sets of spikes. We'll shoot closeups, using metal spikes that really rip up the other guy's spokes. We can shoot those scenes with a car pulling the chariots and nobody onboard. And, we have another set made of rubber for the wide shots." Seigel seemed to be somewhere else for a moment, and then said, "We're shooting a great movie here, a classic. I don't want the mess they had in '25, but we can't let the audience think we've done something cheap. Let me think about this, but I might want a couple of wide shots with the metal spikes. We'll see. Okay, we need to get started on that right away. We don't want to delay shooting."

"I thought I'd take my family to lunch first. I haven't seen these girls for a while, but I'll stop by the props department on our way out and make a sketch for them."

"Be sure to take your family somewhere nice, but remember, we have a schedule to keep."

Yak nodded, and they made their way out the back door, where Tap and Joe waited. Audrea hugged them and said, "Oh, my boys. Let me look at you. I've missed you both so much."

"Well, we've been busy, Mama," Tap answered. "I just went from one movie to another, but I'm not complaining. It's good to have the work."

"You sound like your father. Honey and I went to see that movie as soon as it came out."

"*In Love and in War*," Honey muttered. "What a neat name for a movie."

"It was my first speaking role. I know it wasn't long, but at least they got to see me act a little bit."

"You were good, Tap. I told all my friends about it, but I didn't understand the part about chemical warfare."

"Don't let that bother you," Yak interrupted. "We saw plenty of that in the First World War. It was a cowardly and cruel way to fight, but thank God, people found a better way to kill each other. Uh, that didn't sound right. Anyway, let's go. The hotel is not far, and it has a really good restaurant, that is if you like Italian food."

* * *

Pasta, veal marsala, and fresh bread lay spread over a linen cloth, as the Canutt family sat together for the first time in months. Yakima had reached middle age, and that little, bald spot in the crown of his head had spread to thrice its size. Audrea's red hair showed streaks of gray, but he still saw a reflection of the girl he married in her eyes, and he loved her more than ever. Their boys were adults, and Honey was not far behind them. And, in these quiet moments he realized how much he had missed them.

Audrea took a slice of bread and said, "Did you see the bottles of wine on the other tables? Isn't it a little early for that?"

"Not in Italy," he answered. "I've seen guys drinking at breakfast time. It's just very different here."

"I suppose, but it's strange to me." She looked around the table and said, "Gosh, I'm glad we're all here. We need to do more of this."

"Yes, we do, and I think this is my last time to let them send me somewhere for so long. I didn't want to do it this time, but this movie could be as big as *Gone with the Wind*. Really. And, I don't mind telling you, I can feel the pressure."

"You're a great action director, Sweetheart. If they didn't have confidence in you, Mr. Seigel wouldn't have asked for you."

"I keep thinking about the first *Ben Hur*. The people who did that were geniuses."

"Did they shoot it in Italy?" Tap asked.

"They started in Italy, but they had so many riots and labor strikes that they moved it to Culver City. And, that's where the genius part came in. MGM couldn't afford to build a full-size Colosseum there, so they only built the lower level, like the first bowl of a football stadium without the upper deck."

"But the movie shows people in the upper deck."

"Not really. They hung miniatures on cables with little dolls in them, and they set them closer to the cameras, so it looked like they had a full Colosseum. And, you'll like this Joe. You're the mechanic in the family. The dolls were connected to wooden dowels and motorized cams. They could make them bob up and down, just like the extras when they cheered." Then Honey piped in. "It looked real to me. And, the race looked pretty real too."

"It was. They invited a lot of Hollywood bigwigs to see them shoot the race. They had Mary Pickford and

Douglas Fairbanks and a bunch of other celebrities, but the chariot drivers just sort of paced their way around the track. It was boring. So, one of the directors offered $5,000 to the guy who won the race. Of course, in the movie, Ben Hur wins, but those cowboys drove like crazy." He paused, and his tone turned dour. "And, that's one of the times when things went bad. They raced so hard that they had terrible wrecks, and the drivers around the turn couldn't see them. They hurt a lot of men and killed a lot of horses. But then, that's the way Breezy Eason did things, and they let him do it. Kept every bit of it in the movie."

Audrea took his hand. "You're not Breezy Eason. You'll do fine, and you'll do it without hurting anybody."

"Well, I did learn one thing from Breezy. A stunt is only as good as what the camera gets on film. He had forty-two cameras filming that race. Some were on towers, some hidden in statues, some behind soldiers' shields. He was brilliant at that, and I have to do better. More spectacular stunts and more of them on film. We can't miss a thing."

* * *

Thousands of extras filled the stands, as Yak escorted Audrea and Honey to a bench next to one of the cameras. "You'll get a good view here. Just be sure you don't get excited and step onto the track. You could get run over or get caught by one of the cameras. Remember, they're everywhere, and you're not in the right clothes to be extras."

Trumpets played, and the procession of chariots began. Eleven teams of horses pranced their way around the track, some roan, some gray, with only one team of blacks and one team of whites. Honey stood and said, "Oh, they're so beautiful. And, there's Charlton."

Yak turned to her quickly. "Sit, and try to keep your voice down. Remember the camera is right there." He took the chair next to Audrea and whispered, "Well, we rehearsed this over and over. I guess there's not much I can do now, except sit here and hope it goes well." The teams made several passes around the track, the wide wheels Yak specified skidding around the turns just as he planned. The screams from the crowd made the atmosphere seem festive, but it was all work for Yakima Canutt. "Okay, girls, you can relax a little now. The actors will stop and let the stuntmen take their places."

"Which one doubles who?" Honey asked.

"Tap will replace Stephen Boyd, and Joe doubles Chuck Heston. You might need to hold onto your hat for this scene. It follows a wreck, and there's a chariot on its side near the wall. Now, the chariot we're using has a ramp built into it. Joe's going to run his chariot over that."

"Won't he get hurt?"

"No, baby, not if he does what he's supposed to."
Then he began to do what actions directors must not
do – worry. He waved to his assistant to stop the scene
and then trotted out to Joe's chariot. "I just want to
double check, son."

"You don't need to do that. I'm as ready as I can
be."

Yak tested the reins tied to the front rail. "Okay,
that's good. Now remember, pull the horses up before
you get to the ramp, let them gather themselves. Then
drop the reins and grab hold of the front rail and back
rail."

"I know, I know."

"Then why do you have friction tape in two spots on
the front rail."

"Daddy, if I hold the back rail, then it'll double my
knees and drop me to the floor instead of throwing me
in the air. Holding the front makes for a better gag."
"It also might get you killed, Joe. I had these chariots
specially designed, so they'll slide around the turns.
There's very little room below the undercarriage. If you
fall through the horses, it'll chew you up."
Joe drummed his fingers on the rail and said, "Okay, I
get it. Don't worry."

Yak walked slowly back to his chair, with a churning
in his gut. He wondered whether he should change the
stunt, but he didn't. The crew finished its setup, and
the two Canutt boys brought their teams around the
turn at full gallop, with Joe on the inside. Yak mumbled

as he watched. "Okay, that's good. Good, good. Pull them up, Joe. Pull them up. My God, boy, pull them up." But Joe hit the ramp at full speed with both hands on the front rail, and the impact threw him high and over the front of the chariot onto the reins. His horses made the turn, just as they had been trained, and Joe disappeared on the other side of the spina.

Yak stood and started to run to him, but Audrea caught his arm. "He's a stuntman. Let him do his job. He'll be all right."

"But Audrea . . ."

"No. I've been sitting here praying for my boys, as I always do. Just wait."

His heart was running faster than the horses, but Yak sat down. It felt like a very long time before the chariots rounded the far turn with Joe upright and leading his team of whites. "Oh, Lord Jesus. Thank God."

And Honey said, "Quiet, Daddy. Remember the cameras."

* * *

Dinner came at the same restaurant and at the same table, but this time Yak took a glass of wine. "Are you trying to settle your nerves?" Audrea asked.

"I guess so. If Joe hadn't tied those reins to the chariot, he might've fallen between the horses, and that could've been bad."

"But I didn't fall through, Dad. I just got a little cut on my forehead. I was more worried about Tap's stunt, when he was dragged under the chariot."

"That one didn't bother me. I've done that dozens of times under stagecoaches, but you didn't listen. I told you to pull them up."

"I know, but I thought we would get a better effect, if I hit it full speed."

"Well, don't do that again."

"Don't think?"

"Don't change the gag without talking to me. We haven't injured a single person or animal, and I don't want one of my sons to be the first."

"What about the guy who was run over?" Honey asked. "That scared me to death."

"That wasn't a guy. We built a mechanical dummy for that, but it did look real, didn't it?"

"It sure did." She looked up toward the door. "Oh, Daddy, I forgot."

"Forgot what, baby?"

A lean young man walked to their table. "I invited Tommy to join us for dinner."

He removed his hat and said, "Hello, Mr. Canutt, ma'am. I hope you don't mind."

Yak started to object, but Audrea spoke first. "We don't mind a bit. Why don't you pull a chair from another table and sit by Honey's father and me?"

"Oh, Mama, he's going to sit with me. He's my date, and I don't care if you like it or not."

"I didn't say I didn't like it. I was trying to make him feel welcome."

Dittman sat next to Honey, and the waiter brought him a plate and silverware. "I'd just like a cup of coffee, if that's all right."

Yak rolled his butter knife between his fingers and said, "You know, Tom, one of the reasons I picked you for this job was to get you away from my daughter. I didn't want you fooling around while I was out of the country. And, now here you both are."

"We haven't been fooling around. I'm very fond of Honey. In fact, I think I might love her, but I'd never do anything to shame her or you."

"Yeah? Well, uh, that's good to know. And, you know, I guess that wasn't the only reason I picked you. You're a good stuntman. So, I'm sorry I said that." "I'm not offended. If I was her daddy, I'd be careful about who I let come around too. She's a special girl, and I'd like to see more of her."

"Okay, I guess that could work, maybe. I wanted to talk to you anyway. I've got another stunt for you tomorrow."

"Great. What is it?"

"Do you remember that great big obelisk at the end of the track?"

"Yes, sir. It must be fifty feet high."

"It is, and you're going to ride one of those horses off it. Be sure to roll when you land."

"That's funny." His coffee arrived, and he stirred some sugar into it. "I'll tell you something that's not so funny. I overheard the directors talking today. There's a scene early in the movie, where Messala confronts Ben Hur. They want Stephen Boyd to do that scene like he's a homosexual."

"What?"

"Yeah, they said it would give the audience another reason why Messala hates Ben Hur so much, because of being spurned. But they're not going to tell Mr. Heston about it."

"They'd better not. I've spent a lot of time with Chuck. I don't think he judges people, but he won't stand for being presented that way. He's a man's man and, contract or not, he might just walk. And, if he does, we've done all this for nothing." He paused and then said, "Then again, maybe not. Times are changing."

* * *

The Pantages Theatre looked unimpressive in April, 1960. But for the marquis outside, it could've been mistaken for a cheap hotel on Hollywood Boulevard. Yet it hosted the 32nd Academy Awards, and *Ben Hur* was nominated for twelve Oscars. Among those was one for Charlton Heston for Best Actor. He stood backstage, dressed in a tuxedo and bowtie, listening to the director tell him and the other nominees how much time they had for their speeches, if they won. The group began to break up, with Jack Lemmon and

James Stewart hurrying to their seats, but Heston didn't move. He turned to his left and said, "I wish you'd reconsider, Yak. I'm sure we can find a seat for you on our row."

"No, you made this movie. They only let me stand back here because you made them. I was just hired help."

"You were a lot more than that, my friend. Without you I'd have looked like a guy riding on a merry-go-round. You and that son of yours made me look awfully good. If I win anything tonight, I owe half of it to you."

"It's a great movie, but we knew that when we made it, didn't we?"

"Twelve nominations. I think it'll win Best Picture, but Best Actor? No, I haven't been in the business long enough for that. Oh, yeah, I meant to mention this. We start shooting *El Cid* in a few weeks, and I told the director I want you as Second Unit Director. You'll have full control over all the action scenes, and there are a bunch of them. Well, I'd better get out there. My wife doesn't want to watch the show alone."

Yak stood backstage and watched as *Ben Hur* not only won Best Picture, but ten other Oscars, including Best Actor for Heston. No one applauded Yak or his two sons. But that was his lot as an action director, and he knew it. And, he wondered how great it would be to walk onto that stage just one time.

* * *

Yakima established himself as the premiere second unit director in Hollywood. Movie offers followed one after the other, as quickly as he could handle them. And, his sons moved on to careers of their own. Yak was afraid they would grow distant, but Audrea insisted on regular family dinners. She ordered a new dining table, big enough for two daughters-in-law, Tap's children, and Honey's husband. Sunday afternoon melted into evening. The kids and in-laws had gone home, leaving Yak to his favorite chair and his pipe. "What's bothering you?" he asked.

"Nothing. I'm just thinking."

"Well, you've been pacing around the house for twenty minutes. You look like you've got ants in your drawers."

"The people came to pick up our old table for a charity sale today, and I took them out to the storage building. So, while I was out there, I took a look around, and we need to do something with all your trophies."

"You ain't gonna give them to charity, are you?"

"No, of course not. I think we need a trophy case, a big one. You've got cups and medals and belts scattered all over the place. If we don't organize them, they're going to get damaged or maybe even lost."

"If you're going to do that, start with the *Police Gazette* belts. They kicked off my whole career. Without them, I'd be a used-up, ex-rodeo cowboy."

"No, you wouldn't. You'd have done all right, and so would we." She plopped down on the sofa and said, "I think I'll look through that new catalog and see what they have. Of course, I could go down to Ferguson's. I would like to get this done by the time you get back from Colorado."

"Then you'd better stick with Ferguson's. I'm leaving in the morning, and I won't be gone very long. I expect to shoot all my stuff within a week. By the way, I heard some bad news about Nat King Cole. They say he has lung cancer."

"Oh, that terrible. Are they going to replace him in the movie?"

"I don't think so. They prerecorded the music, so he and Stubby Kaye will lip sync the words for the movie. He's not involved in any of the stunts, so I may not see him at all."

"Well, if you do, tell him I'm praying for him."

"I will. I'm sure he'll appreciate that. While you're at it, say a prayer for me. I hear Jane Fonda is a pistol to work with, but I can understand why. Her mother committed suicide when she was twelve, and that could mess a kid up."

* * *

Only scattered clouds dotted the blue skies over a movie set outside Canon City. Yakima Canutt stood off camera, watching Lee Marvin tremble as a sober Kid Shelleen. The part called for him to fire a shot that missed the target badly and struck a weather vane.

238

Shelleen begged for a drink and said, "It's all over in Dodge, Tombstone too. Cheyenne, Deadwood, all gone. All dead and gone. Why, the last time I came through Tombstone, the big excitement was about the new roller-skating rink they'd laid out over the OK Corral." After downing a pint of whiskey, his nerves steadied, and he fired the rest of his blanks.

The scene ended, and Yak stepped in. "Thanks, everybody. If you'll give us a few minutes, we'll get the shots that go with this scene." He called over the sharpshooter the studio had hired. "Okay, Frank, give me two bullets in the center of the target. Then I need you to shoot that can off the fence and then hit it twice in the air."

Frank raised the gun and fired. He centered the wooden target, but he missed the can. He reloaded and tried again, but still he missed. "What's the deal?" Yak asked. "You're supposed to be good at this.

"I'm trying. It's not easy to hit something in the air, you know. It's probably the wind." His third try was no better than the first two.

Jane Fonda called from off camera, "Maybe he needs a drink."

Yak took the gun and reloaded. He twirled it, like he had done so many times in his silent movies, shot the bottom of the can, tossing it into the air. Then he drilled it twice before it hit the ground. "That's some good shooting," Marvin said.

"I did a lot of hunting when I was young, and well, I do practice." Once he was satisfied his shooting had been captured on film, he stepped aside and sat on the corner of a horse trough.

Within minutes, a slim figure stood beside him. "Thank you for saving the scene."

"Oh, that's all right, Miss Fonda."

"Call me Jane." She sat beside him and crossed one foot over the other. "It's important that we get this movie right. This is my chance to prove I can make it on my own, without depending on my father's name."

"I don't mean to intrude, but I do read up on the principal actors in the movies I work on, and I know you have a tough time with your father."

"Oh, if you only knew. Sometimes, I feel like Kid Shelleen out there, like a need a good, stiff drink."

"Look, I'm nobody special. I'm certainly no doctor or psychologist, but I know something about hard relationships. Lord knows I had one with my first wife, but I hope you and your father can patch things up somehow. I lost my daddy way too early. And, I can tell you this. I saw many a cowboy fall prey to John Barleycorn and drink his way right out of the rodeo business. It ain't the answer."

She seemed to ignore what he said. "Could you teach me to shoot like that?"

"Probably. It does take a steady hand. But we could give it a try in a couple of days, if you like."

"Why not today? We'll be finished here in an hour, and there's plenty of open space."

"This afternoon and tomorrow, I have to teach Lee Marvin to ride a horse. Then I have to show him how to ride one like he's drunk."

"How can you teach him to ride that well in only a day or two?"

"Well, I'll double for him in some scenes, but he'll do enough for people to believe it's him, when it's really me. He's a quick learner."

"And, then what?"

"Then I have to teach his horse how to act drunk."

* * *

After *Cat Ballou*, Yak crossed the ocean again. Egypt was just as hot as he'd heard it would be. He pulled his shirt loose from his sweaty back, only to have it stick again. His friendship with Charlton Heston was only rivaled by his friendship with John Wayne, and now they were working together again on *Khartoum*. Heston wiped away sweat and said, "You know, I almost envy Olivier, sitting up there in England. I need to take lessons from him on how to negotiate a contract."

"Me too," Yak answered. "He must have a lot more clout that we do, but he won't be able to tell his grandchildren about all this sand."

"Well, I guess we should get back to business and stop whining. I've been thinking about this next scene, where I ride my horse behind those rocks."

"Yeah. Joe will be back there to lay the horse down for you."

"Wouldn't it be better if I lay the horse down, and let the audience see that it's me?"

"It's risky. You're the star, and you could get hurt."

"I don't think so. Especially, since Joe showed me how to do it yesterday."

"Joe showed you how? It looks like my boy is going off on his own again. I guess his second unit director needs to have a talk with that young man."

"Don't be too hard on him, Yak. I really pressed him to show me. As you said, I'm the star, so what could he do?"

"He could've come to me, but I don't suppose that matters now. We'll set it up for you."

They walked away together, and Heston asked, "Why are these horses and camels lined up like this?"

"Those are falling horses, and we're going to train the camels to fall, if we can work out a deal with their owners. They don't seem to think we can train them to fall without hurting them. We're going to use soft dirt and mount cushions on their sides. I even told them I'd buy any animal we hurt, but that doesn't seem to be good enough. I don't think they trust me."

"What will you do?"

"I'm going to try something. I noticed one of them carries a whip around. Let's see if he'll loan it to me. I had the prop department drive some posts in the ground and stick some knives in them. Maybe this will work and maybe it won't." He took the whip and snapped it a few times to get the feel of it. Then he snatched all six knives from their posts, but still the owners wagged their heads. So, he tied one of the knives to the end of the whip. "Watch this, Chuck. I did this in a movie once. My character was named Snake, and his favorite way to kill somebody was with a knife and whip." He spread his feet, laid the whip back, and then flipped it with a loud crack. The knife stuck firmly in the wood, and the owners smiled. "Do we have a deal?"

* * *

Yak shot epic battle scenes with thousands of extras attacking the walled city of Khartoum, canon fire from floating galleys, and an exploding bridge. Tap and Joe appeared in many of those scenes, so he took them with him to the screening. "Before we go in, boys, I have something to say. You both did a lot of stunts in this movie, and you made a lot of money, but the company is running short on cash, so the director is looking for someone to blame. I told him we didn't need falls in every battle scene, but he insisted. He knows stuntmen get paid a set amount for each fall, but I guess he just didn't keep count. So, if he brings that up, let me handle it. I don't want one of you losing his temper and maybe also miss out on some movies in the future. Hollywood is a terrible rumor mill. Just hold your tempers."

Joe shrugged and said, "When have we ever lost our tempers?"

"Plenty of times. And, you're the one who worries me more. We'll come through this screening fine, but remember, we've still got a movie to finish, and that means more time in a foreign country. You like to party, Joe, and that can be a problem. This ain't London or even Spain. Egypt is an old country with very old customs. You fool around too much, and they'll stick you in the bottom of one of those pyramids."

"Okay, okay, I'll behave."

"And, one more thing. I know what the film I sent them looks like, but this will be the edited version. We don't get to pick which scenes go into the movie. That's what the director gets paid for. Just watch, and let him do his job."

They found their seats, and the lights dimmed. Yak expected to watch thirty-minutes of film, but he saw less than twenty. When it was over, he stood and said, "I don't know why you brought me all the way over here, if you're just going to water down my scenes like that. You took the action out of action. We'll finish this movie for you, but if that's how you treat my work, don't call me again." No one answered, and the Canutts made their exit.

Heston met them outside. "I hope you don't think I had anything to do with that, Yak."

"No, of course not. But it bothers me when amateurs mess with my stuff."

"Have you seen the clips of Olivier?"
"Yeah, he looks like they painted his face with shoe polish. It reminded me of the blackface minstrel shows from the Thirties. But we're not making a comedy here. It's supposed to be an action movie. I think I've had enough of eating sand for a while. I'm seventy years old, Chuck. I'm getting too old for this nonsense."
"Don't say that. We still need you."

* * *

"Yak, come in. It's too hot for you to be out there cutting grass."

"In a minute. I've still got that stretch behind the barn to do."

Audrea let the screen slam shut, as she called for her daughter. "Honey, go out there and get your daddy."

Her voice rang down the hallway. "I'm changing the baby, Mama."

"I'll do that. He's too old to be out in this kind of heat, and he always listens to you." She met Honey in the hall, who passed by with a coy smile. After a good powdering and fastening a couple of safety pins, she carried her granddaughter to the living room, where Yakima sat with a glass of lemonade. "Good. At least one of us can talk sense to you."

"I guess so. I never could tell that girl no. Here, let me hold that child."

"Not now. You're too sweaty. You can hold her after you've had a shower."

"But Tom will be here by then, and they'll take her home. Come on, give her to grandpa."

Audrea conceded, set her in his lap, and settled into her rocker. "Well, have you given any more thought to retirement? I checked the bank account, and we're doing fine. We don't need the money."

"I've given it a lot of thought. That Academy Award sort of fired me up for a couple of years, but it gets harder and harder to travel around, and I'm really tired of being away from you. If this ain't my last movie, it's going to be close."

"Then, why not just quit now. Tell them to get someone else."

"I would, but it's been a long time since I worked with John, and he's not a kid anymore either. But, if I know him, he'll keep working till he drops. People love the guy, and he can't disappoint his fans. We've got one really big stunt to design, and then I can probably let Tap and Joe do the rest."

"Where are they going to shoot it?"

"Part in Arizona, part in Mexico. Why don't you come with me? Do you remember how we drove through Arizona on our honeymoon?"

"I remember that all right. I was just a young girl, and you took advantage of me."

"Who took advantage of you?" Honey asked, as she entered the room.

"I didn't say someone took advantage of me. I said you father took good care of me."

"Oh. So, Daddy, is Tommy going with you?"

"We already have twenty-one stuntmen for this movie, besides, I thought he was trying to get into production work."

"He is, and he's talking to some people about producing some game shows for TV. I just thought this would give him something in the meantime."

"Your mother and I have been talking about retirement. How would you feel about that?"

"I think it's past time, Daddy. You're supposed to be the action director, but I know you're still doing some stunts. What happens if you break a hip or something? Things don't heal like they did when you were younger, you know."

"Well, there you go. The two women in my life think I'm too old to fall off horses anymore. And, I'm beginning to think you're both right. When we finish *Rio Lobo*, I'll try to stop."

"Do more than try, Daddy."

* * *

He sat in a folding chair next to a railroad track, watching a stunning, chestnut horse trot toward him. Its rider sat tall, dressed in a Civil War uniform. Yakima stood, as they drew near. "My gosh, John, that's a beautiful horse. He reminds me of Tipperary."

"That's why I picked him. I heard this might be your last stunt, and I thought we'd make it special." Wayne dismounted, tied the reins to a tree, and took the chair next to Yak. "Oh, it feels good to sit down, and I don't mean in a saddle."

"I can see why. You're keeping up a pretty good pace lately. Do you remember when we used to shoot a movie every six weeks?"

"Those were the days. We were young bucks back then, not sure if the next movie would be the last or whether the producer might replace us with his cousin or somebody." He groaned and adjusted himself in the chair. "I remember when they used to tell you to put boot black on that bald spot of yours in case your hat fell off while you were doubling me. Now I'm old and fat. And, look at this. They've got me in a toupee."

"Yeah, but it's a good-looking toupee. I thought about a hair piece once, but Audrea talked me out of it."

"How is Audrea, Yak? You know, you really married up when you found her."

"Yes, I did. She's doing real good. Honey's got one child, and we think another might be on the way."

"I know your boys are okay. I saw them climbing into that rail car around the bend."

"They've got some jumps to do from the train. I talked to them and the other stuntmen about that. We designed a safe stunt, but that's a real train coming down those tracks, and those are real trees that it's going to jerk out of the ground. This is no joke."

"I guess we're about to find out. Here she comes."

A pale-yellow boxcar rounded the turn first, followed by a flat car with a cannon mounted to it. They picked up speed, as they raced down the steep incline. Yak moved to the front of his chair. "Looking good, looking good. Now, give her some brakes before you hit the ropes." But the rail cars barreled backwards faster and faster. And, stuntmen began jumping from the boxcar, tumbling down the embankment next to the track. "There goes Tap. Okay, he's clear. Oh, God, I think Joe hit a tree." He wanted to run to him, but Joe sat up and waved that he was all right. Then the yellow car started hitting a series of thick ropes that spanned the tracks, tied on each end to trees. It snapped ropes and uprooted trees by the dozen, slamming them against the sides of the cars. And, finally, the ropes pulled the train cars to a stop. Yak let out a heavy sigh. "Oh, Lord, that one took my breath."

"Mine too," Wayne answered. "I'll say one thing, Yak. If that was your last stunt, you sure going out with a bang."

* * *

The Confederate robbery of the gold train in *Rio Lobo* was Yaks last major stunt. He coordinated a spectacular fight scene for *Breakheart Pass* five years later and served as technical advisor for one other movie, but he knew his best work was done, and he was proud of it. No one recognized him, as he and Audrea walked from the movie studio after watching

The Shootist. Audrea slipped her hand into the crook of his arm and said, "I think that was his best movie."

"Yeah, it was great."

"The scene of Lauren Bacall standing in the window, trying to hold back the tears, was almost too much for me to take. I cried a little." They said nothing more until they reached the car and headed home. "What's wrong, Yak? You seem very quiet."

"The movie is too close to the truth. I meant to tell you before, but I found out this week that John has stomach cancer."

"Oh, God, no."

"It's true. He told me he's enrolling in some kind of vaccine study, but they don't know how much good it will do. I guess, at this point, you try anything."

"Are you okay? I know how much he means to you."

"No, I'm not okay. I've never had a better friend than John Wayne. He's younger than me. I should be the one dying first."

"Don't say that. We don't know God's plans. He gave you to me, and I wouldn't trade you for John Wayne or anybody else."

"I remember what he said one time. He talked about the most important thing being tomorrow. 'It's perfect when it arrives and it puts itself in our hands. It hopes we've learned something from yesterday.' I hope I learned something from my yesterdays, but I'm sure not ready to give that guy up yet."

* * *

To Yakima's regret, Wayne did die first. The Canutt family stood together on a lush hillside at Pacific View Memorial Park, as the casket was lowered into the ground. Honey wrapped her arm around Yak's waist and asked, "What does the inscription on his headstone mean?"

"It's Spanish, and it says 'Ugly, Strong, Dignified.' That's how he saw himself, and that's how he lived. I wish you guys could've known him as a young man. He was so full of life. I never met another person like him."

Audrea sensed her husband had held back his tears as long as he could. She turned to her family and said, "Come on, let's get you daddy home. He's seen enough for one day. We all have."

Yak and Audrea sat in the back of the car, as Tap drove them home. He turned on the radio. "Hey, Mama, do you hear that? It's Willie Nelson, *Don't Let Your Babies Grow Up to be Cowboys*. Do you think maybe he knows something?"

She took Yaks hand in hers and said, "He doesn't know a thing. I say let them all grow up to be cowboys. Those are the ones you love the most."

* * *

Yakima Canutt walked down Vine Street with his cane in one hand and Audrea holding the other. He pressed his cowboy boots into cement, then looked down on his star. He took a moment to reflect *on* people he worked with, those who died or were forgotten, especially from his silent-movie days. He'd won championships, had been admitted to four halls of fame, and walked with the most famous names in Hollywood, but his greatest joy stood around him, family. And, a year later, America's greatest stuntman joined his longtime friend in a place where he would always be young and always be a cowboy.

End

Printed in Great Britain
by Amazon